THE THIRTEENTH OWL

The air was still and heavy and when she got back to her room she opened the window. Then she stretched out on her bed, very weak, and closed her eyes. Immediately she saw the man with the bird head. Standing over the bed like a doctor. But when she opened her eyes she saw nothing.

Not a dream, she thought. I'm wide awake. And there's a sound – a sound in the room.

It was a sound that didn't belong. The hard rustling of plates or tiles settling. Over by the window. Fortune on the ledge, hunched to take off. Moving. Stepping to one side. Stepping back. And rattling his wing tips against the glass.

Imogen sat up slowly. Then, as she was standing, she saw the owl spring.

'No,' she whispered. 'Don't go.'

For Jennifer

I would like to thank colleagues at Bishop Otter College, Chichester, and John Taylor of the BBC, for their help and support.

N.W.

THE THIRTEENTH OWL

Nick Warburton

A Red Fox Book

Published by Random House Children's Books
20 Vauxhall Bridge Road, London SW1V 2SA

A division of Random House UK Ltd

London Melbourne Sydney Auckland
Johannesburg and agencies throughout the world

First published by The Bodley Head Children's Books 1993

Red Fox edition 1994

1 3 5 7 9 10 8 6 4 2

Printed and bound in Great Britain by
Cox & Wyman Ltd, Reading, Berkshire

RANDOM HOUSE UK Limited Reg. No. 954009

ISBN 0 09 922061 X

1

Boy Carter was stubbing stones out of the road with his toe. Imogen watched him through the kiln-room window. The glass was dull with clay dust so she'd smeared a clear circle with her thumb. But Boy Carter was concentrating on his stones. He might not have noticed her anyway. Imogen watched the little clouds of dust swirl up round his ankles; saw him bend and sort out the best sized stones to throw at the school wall. They clicked against the flint and flew off at angles.

'I shan't move while you're there,' Imogen said softly. 'I shan't.'

She turned her back to the window and looked round the kiln-room. The shelves of pots, some fired, some not. The heavy sacks, damp with clay, kicked against the wall – subsiding there like bodies. The dust and muddle of it all. Her father's room, full of her father's work. Some of it had been standing on shelves for years. Never fired. Never quite got round to it. Imogen wouldn't let him move them now, even if it crossed his mind.

'I'd like to go out now,' she said to the empty room. 'Please. I'd like to be outside.'

Behind her, very faint, came the shout of Boy Carter's mother, like an answer to her plea.

'Boy, what are you doing? What are you frittering your time on now?'

No reply from Boy Carter. Just the click of stone on flint.

'Come inside this minute,' his mother shouted. 'Get your lump of a self in here or I'll take your father to you.'

A last stone hit the school wall and the road became silent. Imogen smiled to herself, picturing Boy trailing indoors with his head bowed. Getting a cuff aimed at him for the dust on his boots.

'Cuff him,' she said. 'Cuff him one for me.'

She sighed, lifting her shoulders, and slipped out of the kiln-room into the evening light. But too soon. Just a moment too soon. Boy Carter glimpsed her before he was dragged indoors.

'Crack-pot!' he yelled. 'Where you off to, Crack-pot?'

Imogen turned her back to show she hadn't heard. She hurried down the street, head down like a little old woman.

'Hear me, Crack-pot?' Boy Carter called after her. 'Hear what I say?'

Go in, Boy, she thought. Go in and get your head smacked. And she ran the fingers of her right hand over her cheek. Smooth as an apple and then rough, where the scar was. Her fingers traced the line of the scar.

The potter's daughter. A fair face with a scar down one cheek. Crack-pot, she thought. A little crack-pot.

When she reached the lane outside the village she

slowed. She was by herself, no one at her back, and she felt happier for it. The lane was deep, between two banks of hedge and ivy, and dusk had already reached it. The sky and the fields still seemed light in the late summer air but the lane was closed in with shadow.

She would turn at the first gate and walk the track across Mr Balik's big field. Make her way slowly back and round so that she could come in at the top of the village, and through the snicket by the church. Boy Carter and all the others would be safe inside. You could take the path across Mr Balik's field. You were allowed to do that. He didn't like it. Sometimes he was working in the fields when Imogen walked past and he stopped what he was doing to watch her walk by. Whenever he was there she pulled her shawl round her head and didn't look to one side or the other. But she always felt him there, pausing in his work, watching her. Making sure that her feet remained on the track and didn't stray on to his land.

Tonight there was no sign of him. Or anyone else. Imogen liked it best like that. Herself treading the ground, the light draining out of the sky, Old Carter's dog barking far away in the village. Probably barking at Boy who was probably aggravating the poor thing. And Boy maybe getting nipped for it.

She began to sing to herself. The crop had been harvested and Imogen passed between two seas of stubble. Her track was marked by the solid prints of work horses, dried in the sun. It cut straight through the field and ended at a clump of old trees. The trees were in a dip to the left, with several ways through them and back on to the upper road at the top of the village. On the right was a blackened barn in the corner of Mr Balik's field. It sagged at one end, as if it had a weight on the roof.

Imogen stopped walking and turned a slow circle on the spot. Looking back at the path she'd walked, then at the twisted trees, and at the barn, moving steadily across her vision as she turned.

Then she saw it.

The owl. Short and upright on a branch which reached towards her like an arm. Watching her. Because of the dip down to the trees it was almost at eye-level. She caught her breath and stopped turning. For a long second they looked at each other.

Imogen, pale and still. The owl steady, a light, glowing brown, its feathers flecked. Imogen's blue eyes narrowed, so she could see all there was of the owl. The owl's eyes black, darker than the dark trees behind it.

The owl hunched to take off. It fell from the branch and swooped down, then up and off to Imogen's right. Its wings were white underneath, both soft and hard, curved like flexing swords in the dusk. It flew in complete silence towards the barn, flickered for a moment and then disappeared somewhere into the roof. Imogen stood and watched the barn until parts of it had faded into the general darkness. But the owl could not be seen again. It was in there somewhere, a fierce life waiting on some beam or ledge. Alone in the barn.

Dad spooned stew into their brown bowls. The

bowls were seconds, imperfect, for home use only. The best pots went to the shop for others to buy.

'What's to do this evening, Imogen?' he asked her.

'I don't know. I was thinking, maybe I could make something. From a bit of left-over.'

'Left-over stew?' he said, lifting an eyebrow but not smiling. 'I can't see that there'll be any.'

'Not stew, you soft thing. A bit of clay.'

'Oh, clay. Ay, well make it small and perhaps I'll fit it in the kiln. As long as . . .'

'As long as it's good enough,' said Imogen. 'I know.'

'Do you want to be in on an evening like this?' he asked her.

'I don't mind.'

'You've not been out all day.'

He looked up from his bowl. He didn't make much effort to persuade Imogen to go out but sometimes he thought about it. And she knew he did.

'I was out before supper, Dad. Didn't you miss me?'

'Oh,' he said. 'Of course you were.'

'I took a walk over Mr Balik's field.'

'By the track, I trust. You don't want to meddle with that dry old stick.'

No one in the village wanted to meddle with Mr Balik. Although there were occasions when they had to. When Mr Balik or his man, Grainger, came for the rents. When he also had a good look round, to check that all was in order.

'Of course by the track,' said Imogen.

'And what did you see?'

'What I usually see. The field. The barn. The usual things.'

Something stopped her telling him about the owl.

After supper Imogen took the oil lamp into the kiln-room and sat herself at one of the benches. She took two or three pinches of clay and worked them between her fingers. The clay was squeezed into a face, an apple, a round-bodied rabbit, but none of these things was satisfactory. She rolled it into a ball again. A crust dried on her hands and she clapped it off, then sat looking at the shapeless lump for a while, wondering how it would end up.

When she started again she had no clearer idea of what it was going to be but gradually it turned itself into a little dragon with lifted wings, its body arched as if it was about to spring.

Then she heard her father's boots scrape over the threshold.

'Imogen,' he said, stepping into the pool of light from the oil lamp. 'It's getting late.'

'Well, I've done all I'm doing tonight,' she told him.

He squatted down and looked closely at the dragon.

'Eh, it's fine, is that,' he said. 'A lizard, is it?'

'A dragon, of sorts.'

'It'll do nicely, Imogen. We can find a bit of kiln space for that, I'm sure.'

She was pleased. Dad didn't put things in the kiln unless they deserved their place. And she liked to see him satisfied with what she'd done. But the little dragon itself she wasn't so happy about. It was all right, but that was all.

She wrapped it in a damp cloth and decided to

leave it overnight. See how it looked in the morning. She was sure, though, that she would squeeze it into a ball and start again. Or maybe give up making something this time round. She liked what she made to be perfect and the shape under the cloth wasn't the thing she'd had in mind. This time, though, she couldn't really grasp what that thing was supposed to be.

2

Imogen had no chance to go back to the dragon in the morning. Instead she went with her father to collect wood for the kiln. They went round the back of Old Carter's cottage and Dad sawed up good lengths from the fallen apple tree while Imogen loaded them on to the handcart. There was no sign of Boy but that didn't mean anything. There was no sign that he was far away either.

Boy was easy to avoid when school was on. He had little to say to Imogen and rollicked around with the other boys during play. That was safe enough. And she could sit in her desk during lessons and do her work, with the cracked side of her face angled away to the edge of the room. Mr Popplewell never said anything about it. He never had done, and whenever he looked at Imogen he pretended he couldn't see any scar. Even though she could see in his eyes that he had.

During the long holidays, though, you couldn't be sure where Boy might lurk. You might go for days without seeing him, and then he'd give a whole afternoon to following her around. Taunting her for a reaction like he sometimes did to the dog. He was a year or two younger than Imogen but a world away in sense, she thought.

When the cart was full, Old Carter came out of the cottage to collect the payment from Dad. He wasn't really old. He was probably about thirty. Tall with a red face and sandy hair. They only called him Old Carter after Boy was born and his wife insisted on calling the child Carter too.

'I won't ask much,' Old Carter said. 'The tree's come down and I don't want it cluttering the yard. You're doing me a favour.'

But he made sure he asked for something. And Dad was content to pay, though he kept quiet about how well it suited him. The apple was good, slow-burning wood. It would do nicely for the kiln. And both he and Imogen liked its smell when it burned.

'Come and have something to drink,' Old Carter said when the price was paid. He led the way into the cottage, stooping at the kitchen door and holding his hand out behind him to indicate that Dad should follow.

Imogen hesitated in the yard. She wasn't sure that Old Carter meant her to come in and have a drink. He had a way of not noticing she was there. She went over to the handcart and tidied the apple branches so that they shouldn't fall on the way back to the kiln-room. A pointless job – thc rearrangement made them no more secure – but she didn't feel comfortable about standing still in the yard and doing nothing. When she'd finished she sat down with her back to the dog's kennel.

Old Carter's wife engaged herself in a rattling conversation with Dad, complaining about the weather, the dog and Boy. Their voices drifted into the yard.

Then Boy and the dog came scuttling round the side of the cottage and stopped in their tracks at the sight of Imogen. She stared at Boy for a moment and then turned away. He was not looking into her eyes but at her cheek.

'What you doing here, Crack-pot?' Boy asked.

'What's it look like?'

'It looks like nothing.'

'I'm collecting wood.'

Boy walked up to the hand cart and jiggled the branches around.

'This is our tree,' he said.

'Not now it isn't,' Imogen told him. 'It's our kindling. Bought and paid for so keep your fingers to yourself.'

She was prepared to swipe him one. Hoping he might do something that asked for a swipe. He came up to her and dropped to the ground, resting on his elbow and still gawping at her face. The dog nosed Imogen's knee and slunk into its kennel.

'What you staring at, Snotty?' she said.

'How'd'you get that?'

'Mind your own.'

'Does it hurt?'

He was looking at her without taunting this time. Just curious. Imogen felt like an insect on a leaf. She put her fingers to her cheek to cover the scar.

'I only want to know,' said Boy.

It was probably the nearest he'd ever been to her.

'I burnt it,' she told him simply.

'How?'

'On the kiln door.'

She remembered. Three years old, following Dad around in the kiln-room. Stumbling over his feet and falling against the kiln door which was open to take out the pots. The searing pain. And her ears filled with the sound of her own frightened scream.

'How can you burn yourself on a door?' asked Boy.

'It's white hot in a kiln. You have to have a glove for a kiln door. Don't you know that?'

Dad had whisked her off her feet and squeezed her to him, cursing the kiln and himself over and over.

Boy Carter sat up frowning and leaned towards her. He put his hand up and tried to touch her cheek. As if Imogen wasn't there. Not a person at all.

'No!' she yelled, twisting her head away.

And she swiped at him. Her fingers snatched up dust and sprayed it in his eyes. Her knuckles clicked against his nose. Boy yowled and looked down at the warm blood dripping on to his palms. There was a clattering of feet behind her and Dad and Old Carter appeared at the kitchen door. Wiping their mouths and blinking in the sunlight.

Dad hadn't said much about Boy's bloodied nose. Perhaps he knew the reason for it. Boy's mother had shaken him into the kitchen to put his head in a bowl. She said he'd probably asked for it but you couldn't tell from her cross face what she was really thinking.

In the evening, when Imogen went out into the lanes, she found herself remembering the owl. She turned towards Mr Balik's field, and half hoped that it might be there again, peering into the stubble for prey. She pictured its talons, fixed on the branch. The sharpness of death. They talked about that in church sometimes. About overcoming the sharpness of death.

As she approached the clump of trees where she'd seen her owl, Imogen slowed down. She thought she could discern a pale blur moving against the dark background towards the barn. She couldn't be sure, though. Voices came to her over the field. There were men, down in the corner by the barn. She quickened her step.

Two men, bending and shifting around at the base of the old barn. Grainger, the land manager, in his faded smock, silent and busy as usual. And Mr Balik himself. They were so intent on what they were doing that they didn't notice Imogen. She stopped to watch them.

Grainger was leaning loose bundles of sticks and straw against the barn wall. At first Imogen thought they were trying to prop the old building up. It sagged like a tired bullock and maybe the walls needed some extra support. But not with straw. Straw could only be for another purpose.

'Be a bit sharp, man,' Mr Balik was saying. 'I want this done tonight, not tomorrow.'

Grainger's reply was mumbled into the shadows. He lifted a foot and trod the bundles into place.

'They're going to burn it,' Imogen said quietly to herself. Then shouted out loud.

'No!'

Mr Balik looked up and saw a girl running across the corner of the field towards him. Her fair hair swished from side to side as she ran. Her feet crunched on the stubble.

'No!' she was shouting. 'You can't!'

'What is all this?' he said.

Imogen hurtled into him and clutched his arm to stop herself falling. He shook her off.

'Take your hands off me, girl. What are you doing on my land?'

'You can't burn the barn, Mr Balik,' she said.

'Can't? Who's telling me I can't?'

She looked up into his face which was silhouetted against the sky. His black hair, long and straight, was swept behind his ears where it hung on to his shoulders. He wore a shirt without a collar. A point of gold shone from a stud by his neck.

'I'm sorry, Mr Balik,' Imogen gasped. 'I didn't mean to stray off the track . . .'

'Then you can get back on it. Now.'

'But you don't understand . . .'

He took hold of her wrist and shook her. She would've fallen if his grip hadn't been so firm.

'What do you mean, I don't understand? What are you saying? You come running across my field, telling me I don't understand.'

'No,' she said. 'It's the barn. There's an owl . . .'

But she was too frightened to say properly what she meant. She looked at Grainger, hoping for a word of help from him, but he was bent over one of the bundles. Stopped in the middle of his task, watching Imogen and waiting to see what Mr Balik intended next.

'Please, Mr Balik, don't turn the barn.'

'Good God. I'll burn what I like on my own land.'

'But there's an owl. I saw it flying . . .'

'I want to hear no more. Do you understand, girl? Have you got it clear?'

She took a sharp breath, to stop herself crying, and she couldn't do that and speak. So she simply stared up at Mr Balik and then flinched as his hand darted towards her. He caught her by the jaw, squeezing her till her lips bunched.

'You are on my property,' he said. 'Trespass.'

His hand was large and calloused. He lowered his head to look into her eyes. Imogen saw him open his mouth to speak again. And then hesitate. A cloud of doubt seemed to pass over his face. With a turn of his wrist he twisted her head round, studying her. Whatever he intended to say dried in his throat. For a second the anger disappeared. Then he shoved her away so that she fell backwards on to the stubble and he strode back towards the barn.

'What are you waiting for, man?' he barked at Grainger. 'Get it going!'

Grainger came to life and pushed home the last bundle of sticks with his foot. He took matches from his smock and flicked his wrist to strike one. Yellow flames were sucked into the straw.

Imogen picked herself up and scrambled away, back towards the track. By the time she turned, the flames had taken hold and were licking up to the roof. She stood helplessly watching as the fire cracked and pulled the barn down into its heart. There were blackened ribs against the wall of flame and specks of dark floating into the sky. Smoke folded down into the field and drifted towards her. Her eyes were stinging but she blinked to clear them and focus on those specks. Trying to make out something from the way they moved.

But she couldn't tell. They just looked like specks and there was no life in them.

That night, Imogen loitered in the kiln-room before going in to see Dad. She took a pot and scooped some water from the barrel in the yard. Her eyes were red from smoke and crying and she dabbed at them until they felt fresh. There were also parallel scratch marks on one arm. They must've been caused by her fall in the stubble but she hadn't noticed them until she got home. She was about to cross the yard into the kitchen when she caught sight of the cloth over the little dragon.

'You're not right, are you?' she said, peeling back the cloth. 'Poor thing.'

And she squeezed it into shapelessness again. She saw why it wouldn't do. It was trying to become something it shouldn't be. It shouldn't be a dragon but an owl. Now that she understood that, Imogen wanted to work on it immediately, before this day was over. To work uninterrupted.

But first she had to see Dad. She didn't want him to come looking for her.

The evening passed quietly. When she went up to her room, she lay awake until she heard Dad's tread on the stairs up to the loft. She waited another half hour and then she took the faded grey cloak from the back of her door. Her mother's cloak. Her mother, who was no more to her than a soft brown photograph on the mantlepiece. She held the cloak to her face for a moment and then pulled it round her shoulders and went barefoot to the kiln-room.

The whole village was in darkness. Not that it mattered to Imogen. Outside her circle of lamp-light it could have been bright daylight and she wouldn't have noticed. She heard the church clock chime one, then, what felt like a short time later, half-past. And she was standing back from the bench, looking at the owl she had made, feeling it was still not right, when the clock chimed again. Three o'clock.

She turned her back on her work and walked outside. The air was black, almost trembling with unseen life. She waited. Perhaps an owl would call to her. Perhaps the sound of it would make her finish the figure as she knew it must be finished. But there was no owl. Almost no sound at all. It was as if the night were mourning the loss of all owls.

She remembered her own owl, staring at her and hunching to take off. Fierce and wild. Like a cold white flame. She remembered the panic she felt at the sight of the burning barn. That wall of flame.

When she returned to the bench she took up one of the modelling sticks and gouged roughly at the figure's eyes. Two deep holes, imperfectly round. And there it stood. Tiny and red, a piece of solid clay. But with a new life of its own.

3

She woke late the following morning and went straight to the kiln-room to look at her owl again. She feared it might seem lifeless in the daylight. Dad was there ahead of her, cradling it in his palm.

'What happened to your dragon?' he said.

'I didn't like it. I had to make that instead.'

'You were right to change your mind, Imogen. This is better. I'm proper proud of it.'

After the owl had been fired, Dad took it into the shop and stood it in the middle of the shelf in the big window.

'Will someone want it, do you think?' Imogen asked.

'Someone is bound to.'

'To buy it?'

'To buy it, certainly. And the pennies shall be all yours.' He turned from the window and smiled at her. 'It's your work and I'm a fair master, I hope,' he said.

'I don't know, Dad. It might not be right . . .'

'Of course it would. Boy's mother would love that. It'd go with her china pieces over their fire-place.'

Imogen looked at the owl and frowned.

'I don't think I'd like it, though,' she said.

'Boy won't go near it, sweet. He wouldn't dare.'

'It's not that. I don't think I want it to go out of the home.'

'No? Well, maybe it would be hard to say good-bye to it. We'll show it, then, shall we? Show it but not sell it. Eh?'

And he made a card to prop beside it: not for sale.

For several days Imogen did not go out to walk across the fields in the evenings. Didn't stop to watch the birds, didn't sing to herself. The country-side outside the village was no longer a place to go to be alone. She feared that kind of loneliness now. Now she thought of those fields as a place of drifting smoke and sudden violence. A kind of smoke drifting through her own head.

She said little, kept her thoughts to herself. And nobody noticed the difference in her. She was silent, sometimes looking thoughtful. Well, that couldn't really be called a change. That was the way she was. So the difference stayed hidden from others.

At night, those moments in which the barn caught fire came back to her. She saw the broad face of a white owl, looming from side to side, inches away from her eyes. And behind it the flames, forcing it towards her.

Sometimes she saw the owl as she remembered it. A fleeting, silent figure. But at other times it came to her as the little clay figure she'd made. Curiously alive and hovering before her with a rattling of stiff wings. And she would wake and stare into the dark corners of her room. As if she expected it to be perched there somewhere, watching her.

'What is it?' she would ask softly. 'What do you want?'

She listened to the sounds of the night, straining to hear a settling of feathers in the dark.

'I can't help you now,' she said. 'It's too late.'

And when she slept again the owl would return. Sometimes living feather and talon, sometimes the curious, seeing clay. These dreams disturbed her because she hardly knew what they meant. But she wasn't frightened by them.

One night she crept downstairs to the shop. She took her clay owl off the shelf and held it in her fingers. The life it had was what she'd given it. Nothing more. But it comforted her.

'Fortune,' she said. 'I'll call you Fortune.'

Dad was somewhere out in the yard and Imogen thought she could hear the shop bell. She came through to the shop to see but it was empty. She ducked under the counter and went to the big window to peer between the displayed pots. Mr Balik was coming down the street with Grainger trailing a yard or two in the dust behind him. She saw at once it was Mr Balik, his black hair swept back from his high, palc forehead, and she caught her breath. She thought perhaps he'd come to complain about her trespassing the other evening; to find out what must be done about it.

There was hardly anyone else about. Very likely people were staying indoors till the two men had passed. Mr Balik wasn't the sort of man you exchanged pleasantries with. You lived on his land and paid him for it. You didn't stop to chat.

Only one other figure remained in the street. Boy Carter, kneeling by his front step and playing with some mud he'd made. Imogen saw Boy look up, take notice of the dark figure striding down the middle of the road towards him, then carry on playing. She saw him toss little balls of mud into the road. His mouth pouted and opened as he watched them explode.

Imogen was turning away, into the shadows of the shop, when an unexpected movement stopped her. It was Boy, swinging his arm up in a peculiar gesture as Mr Balik and Grainger drew level with him. There was a moment of stillness. Boy was looking up at Mr Balik, squinting with a wide grin into the sun. Then Mr Balik stooped and rubbed something off the toe of his boot with one thumb, and Grainger stepped forward, to give Boy a rough word and send him packing.

But he was prevented. Mr Balik stood sharply and his stick whipped through the air, stinging into Boy's calf. Imogen heard the smack. Another moment of stillness, the squint still frozen on Boy's face.

Briefly, Imogen laughed to herself. He was getting what he'd asked for many, many times. For his silly pranks and stupidity. But the stick was lifted again, high, as if Mr Balik intended more hurt, and Boy tried to make himself small in the road. Frightened, not understanding, Imogen was shocked. Without thinking, she started forward, one hand reaching for the door to the street. But Grainger had stepped between Mr Balik and the boy. He took the stick from his master's hand, quite slowly and gently. Then handed it back to him. Mr Balik took it and immediately turned away. He continued to walk steadily down the street, towards the potter's shop.

This time Imogen did shrink back into shop, darting under the counter and into the safety of the middle room where she could watch through a crack in the door. Half a minute later Mr Balik pushed into the shop. The bell jangled in the silence and Imogen thought it took far longer than usual to fade away. She held her breath and watched Mr Balik.

She was surprised to see how impassive his face looked. As if he'd strolled down from the big house and nothing had interrupted his progress.

No one came to the sound of the bell so Mr Balik turned to the window and lowered his head to the glass. He looked into the street for a moment or two before his attention was caught by something on one of the shelves. He had his back to Imogen. A broad back, bent as he examined whatever it was that he'd seen. His hands, one of them holding that same stick – Imogen could now see that it had a silver top – rested on his hips. After a moment he straightened and turned, impatiently, looking into the shadows to see if anyone was coming to speak to him. Imogen took a step back and cowered behind the door.

'Shop!' called Mr Balik. 'Where are you, then?'

He rapped his stick on the floor and went back to looking at the things on the shelves. Dad came hurrying from the back.

'Didn't you hear the bell?' he asked Imogen in a hushed voice as he pushed by.

Before she could answer, Dad had continued into the shop and seen that it was Mr Balik calling for him. He wiped his hands on a scrap of towelling and dropped it on to the floor behind him.

'Mr Balik,' he said. 'I'm sorry. I didn't know it was you.'

'I've come for rent, potter. Not to buy.'

'Yes, of course,' said Dad. He called to Imogen over his shoulder. 'Imogen. Fetch the jar, will you, sweet?'

Mr Balik's gaze pierced the gloom and found her out. His face remained expressionless, though. He did not seem to know her. Relieved, she ran into the kitchen to get the money jar. When she returned, Mr Balik was squatting down by the window, tapping his stick against his knee.

'Now I'm here, though,' he was saying, 'I do see something that I like.'

'Yes, sir?'

'But it says "not for sale". So, what can be done?'

Imogen held her breath. Why was Mr Balik looking at her owl? Did he know more about it than he showed in his face? Perhaps he recognized her after all. Remembered the wild girl who shouted at him about owls. And maybe this was a twisted way of bringing the subject up.

'I'm afraid I couldn't sell that, sir,' Dad said as he counted coins out of the jar. 'It's not mine, you see.'

'Really?'

Mr Balik flicked another glance in Imogen's direction. But, again, she could see no recognition in his face.

'No, it's my daughter's and she wants to keep it,'

Dad went on. 'So she says. Although I suppose I could . . .'

'No. Let her keep it,' said Mr Balik, pursing his lips.

Dad handed the money to Mr Balik who nodded briefly and turned for the door.

'I could make another, if you like,' Dad said.

'Another? Just like this.'

'As like as I can get it, Mr Balik. Or bigger. I could make a large one for you.'

For a moment Mr Balik stood still and said nothing. He held the shop door open with his stick and loosened a strand of hair from his collar with one finger.

'Yes,' he said softly, almost to himself. 'Yes, make me one like that. Life size.'

'Life size, sir?'

'In fact . . .' He looked up at Dad. 'Make me more than one. A dozen. Can you do that?'

'A dozen? Of course, Mr Balik. Of course.'

'Good. Let me know when they're ready.'

And he left the shop, clattering the door behind him.

Dad's eyes were shining. He looked round for Imogen and smiled broadly at her. A dozen owls for Mr Balik. She couldn't remember him ever getting a job like that before and she was pleased that her little owl had helped it come about.

'Tell me what I just heard, Imogen,' said Dad. 'Twelve owls for Mr Balik. Is that what he said?'

'It is, Dad. Will he pay well?'

'Oh, he will, sweet. He's very fair about such matters, whatever else you might say about him. I think we're about to make our fortune, you and I.'

But beneath his delight at the work, Imogen thought she detected a worry in Dad's eyes. If she hadn't known his face so well she wouldn't have noticed it. That hint of anxiety. I'm not sure I can do it. I'm not sure I can get it right.

4

Throughout the rest of the week, Imogen and her father worked hard on Mr Balik's commission. Dad kneaded the clay and built up the bodies in careful layers. Imogen concentrated on the details, returning to each figure again and again until she was satisfied that it looked right. She had little need to go back to her original owl, though. The image of that was fixed firmly in her mind. At first, Dad wouldn't trust her to do the modelling from her head. He wanted her to keep checking and sometimes, when his part of the work was done, he watched nervously over her shoulder.

'He'll want them exact, Imogen,' he told her. 'It won't do if they're any different.'

'Don't worry, Dad,' she said. 'They're all right.'

'But there's a lot to go wrong, sweet. There's the firing, for a start. The more I think about that the more it worries me.'

'Then we must make another one.'

'Another one?'

'Yes,' said Imogen, concentrating on the clay beneath her fingers. 'We must make thirteen. One for luck. Just in case.'

And that's just what they did.

When they were finished and lined up on the bench in the kiln-room, Imogen told her father to go out into the yard and worry there for a moment or two. She took a piece of wire and scratched a number at random on the base of each one.

'Now, potter,' she said sternly when she led her father back into the kiln-room, 'which is the thirteenth owl? Can you find him for me?'

He frowned and moved slowly down the line, studying each one in turn. He hesitated over first one and then another.

'This one?' he said at last.

'No,' smiled Imogen. 'That's number five. But it wouldn't matter. They're all the same. Twins, or whatever you call thirteen identical owls.'

He laughed at her, standing there so proudly beside her line of owls. He was almost relaxed. But she knew he wouldn't be truly at ease until they were all fired and delivered safely to Mr Balik's house.

'I'm going to sit by this kiln until I know for sure,' he said.

'That's going to be a long wait, Dad.'

'Well, I shan't sleep if I leave them to it so I might as well be in here.'

He took a chair from the kitchen and settled himself beside the kiln. Sideways to the door so he could hear the fire purring to itself. Imogen went back to the house and attended to the shop until closing time. It was a quiet afternoon with few customers. Mr Bailey, the man from The Hope, called to collect three jugs he'd ordered. Boy Carter came lurking outside the window but ran off as soon as Imogen got to her feet and took a step towards the door.

At dusk she locked up and turned the sign round to show they were closed. Then she took her little owl off its shelf and carried it through to the kitchen. She stood it on the window ledge while she cut Dad some bread and cheese and heated him some milk. She placed the food and drink on a wooden tray with the owl. When she took these things out to him, she saw Dad with his head nodding on his chest and the lids of his eyes sliding shut.

'Let me sit here awhile,' she said. 'Nothing will go wrong. And, if it does, I'll know what to do about it.'

'It if goes wrong, Imogen,' Dad said, hauling himself stiffly from his chair, 'you're to call me. At once. Do you understand?'

'Of course I understand. Go inside and rest.'

Alone in the kiln-room, Imogen didn't feel like sleeping. She thought she'd been tired but now found that she was wide awake. She turned the little owl over and over in her hands, thinking of nothing in particular. She looked into the dark holes of its eyes as it turned, and ran her fingers over the curve of its wings.

Then, without warning, she felt it move in her hand.

A tiny pulse of life, as if it was wriggling to be free. She caught her breath and watched it slip through her fingers and dash against the stone floor, exploding in fragments.

Before the shock hit her, she heard another sound. Nearby. A rattling whisper this time, from the kiln.

'Dad,' she said fearfully, but not loud enough for anyone to hear.

The rattling sound came again. And, yes, it was inside the kiln. Imogen picked up the heavy glove Dad used to open the door. She knew she shouldn't do it, knew that the thirteen owls were in the middle of firing. But she had to look. She had to see what was making that noise.

The door swung open for only a moment or two. Imogen glimpsed a block of yellow-white light, broken by the huddled shapes of the dark owls. A fierce heat wafted against her face and she screwed up her eyes to peer into its heart. There was no movement in the kiln. Only sound. That same whisper of a rattle, louder now that the door was open. It was dying on a hiss when a second explosion jumped out at her. A violent crack, deeper and more resonant than the smashing of Fortune.

She slammed the door shut and stepped backwards. Then she ran. Out of the kiln-room and away. Anywhere that was away from that terrible, live rattling sound and the crack that meant that she had maybe ruined Mr Balik's owls.

'Imogen? Imogen, are you awake?'

She was curled up on her bed. Dad was looking down at her.

'I thought you were in the kiln-room,' he said. 'I thought you were still watching.'

She sat up and looked around. Strong morning light was coming into the room. Everything seemed peaceful and ordinary. Boy Carter's small voice was shouting outside somewhere. And his dog was barking back at him.

'You should've woken me, Imogen. If you were tired I'd've carried on watching. I didn't want those owls left by themselves.'

'I got frightened . . .' she said.

'Frightened?'

'Yes, but . . .'

She stopped herself. She didn't mean to tell him what she'd heard but she found she was speaking about it before she was fully awake.

'What was there to be frightened of?'

'Nothing. No . . . It was just dark and . . .'

'Well, it doesn't matter, sweet. The firing's done and your owls are all out on the bench.' He paused and smiled at her. 'And they're fine, Imogen. Every one of them.'

'They're all right?'

'Perfectly. And waiting for you to inspect them. Are you coming?'

He took her down to the kiln-room, bubbling with chatter and relief, and stood aside so she could step in first. The owls were ranged on the bench. A perfect line in the dusty light. Not destroyed, as Imogen had feared. She felt like singing at the sight of them.

'Now,' said Dad, 'here they are. Take a good look at them, young potter, and tell me which one is number thirteen. Pick him out for me.'

She smiled and moved slowly down the line, just as he had done before the firing. Each one was solid and true and as like its brothers as made no difference. Until . . .

A face with a crack across it.

The same deep eyes as the others, the same turn

of its head, but a thin crack running diagonally down one side of its flat face.

Imogen stopped and turned back to her father. Surely he knew that one of the owls was cracked? But no. He was still smiling at her. Nodding slightly and smiling in anticipation. To him they were all alike. She reached out her hand, as if to touch the damaged figure, and hesitated. Then she moved on, two places down the line.

'This one?' she said.

She looked at Dad and tried to match his smile.

'No,' he said. 'Or maybe yes. I can't tell. You must look at the numbers on the back.'

The number on the back said nine which seemed to delight him even more. Imogen knew what the number on the cracked owl would be.

5

On the Tuesday morning, Dad wheeled the hand-cart to the front of the shop and they loaded the owls to take to Mr Balik. They put a layer of straw in the bottom of the cart and packed more straw, like blankets, round each of the figures. Dad's face was shining with sweat and concentration as he carried them from the shop to the cart.

'Will he like them, Dad, do you think?' Imogen asked him.

'He can't fail to like them. They're just what he asked for. Twelve fine owls.'

'Thirteen.'

'That's right. Thirteen. Enough for a judge and a jury.'

He breathed deeply and wiped his hands on his trousers. Then he began to push the cart carefully up the hill towards the big house. Imogen walked ahead to warn of holes in the road or chickens which might take it into their heads to dart under the wheels. Several people stopped what they were doing to watch the cart go by. Mr Bailey appeared at the doorway of The Hope with one of Dad's jugs in his hand.

'Where to with that lot, potter?' he called.

'To Balik's,' Dad said without taking his eyes off the road.

When they reached the church there was a flurry of movement somewhere to their left and Boy Carter erupted from the snicket. Dad heaved the handles of the cart round. Boy's mouth gaped with shock and he stumbled over his own feet as he tried to swerve clear. He charged into the side of the cart with his head and shoulders. The cart lurched, balanced on one wheel for a second and dropped down again with a shudder. Boy toppled backwards into the dust. There was a moment's silence while the three of them looked at each other.

'Oaf!' said Dad through his teeth. 'Bloody little oaf!'

It was the first time Imogen heard him call anyone bloody or oaf. She was more startled by that than by Boy's tumbling out of the snicket so unexpectedly. It sounded wrong, even though she knew Boy was all the things Dad had called him.

Dad lowered the handles of the cart and started delving in the straw. He had to step over Boy who was sitting upright in the road and had started blubbering to himself. All those times she'd willed him to hurt himself, to fall off walls and be cuffed by his mother; now that he was here at her feet, wailing like a baby, it didn't seem to mean very much. There was no satisfaction in it.

She ran up to him and pulled him to his feet. It was the first time she'd been close to him since Mr Balik had beaten him in the street. He was wearing coarse trousers, cut off at the knee, and, as she held him firmly by the elbows, she was able to look closely at the back of his legs. He sagged in her grip. She could see none of the marks she'd been imagining, only streaks of dust on a brownish skin.

'Are you all right?' she asked, meaning the beating but knowing he wouldn't understand. Then she hissed at him, 'Get off. Get yourself off home while you've the chance.'

At the sound of her voice he stopped blubbering and looked up. He blinked, then tried to pull away from her.

'Go on,' she said, shaking him. 'Unless you want to stay here and see what happens next.'

Without another sound he scuttled off towards the Carters' cottage and was well out of the way by the time Dad turned round from the cart.

'Where is he?' he asked.

His face was pale and shiny. He clenched his fists.

'He's run off. Is there any damage, Dad?'

'Not that I can see. But I'm not taking them out for a proper look. Not here in the road. Not with mad ragbags like him about.'

'He didn't mean it,' said Imogen. 'That's just Boy. He's always running his head into something or other.'

'Well, he ought to think before he moves.'

'I'm not sure he's able to, Dad. Let's get these up to Mr Balik's while we can, shall we?'

They left the handcart at the foot of the broad steps up to Mr Balik's door. Grainger let them in. He was expecting them.

'No,' he said shortly, 'I know why you've come, though I don't know who put it into your heads.'

He turned his back and allowed them to follow

him across the hall. It had a marble floor of black and white squares and the air was cool and full of soft shadows high above their heads. Three sets of tall doors led to the rest of the ground floor. One stood ajar, revealing a cream-grey corridor which Imogen found unbearably gloomy. To their left a staircase with iron posts and handrails swept away to a landing and the upper rooms.

When it looked as though they were about to follow him through one of the double doors, Grainger cleared his throat and barred the way.

'Wait here,' he said. 'Mr Balik will come to you.'

He backed through the double doors and pulled them to with a soft click which echoed off the marble.

Dad looked at Imogen and smiled nervously. He wiped his lips with the back of one finger and she thought he looked afraid to break the silence.

'You've brought the owls?'

Speaking before they knew he was there, Mr Balik was striding into the hall in riding boots which clicked over the floor.

'I'll see them now,' he said. 'Where are they?'

'In the handcart, Mr Balik. Outside,' said Dad.

'Bring it in. Grainger, help them. I'd like them all out on the floor.'

Grainger and Dad hurried out to the cart and eased it slowly up the steps. A block of sunlight fell into the hall as Grainger unbolted the tall front door. The light struck Mr Balik, making him narrow his eyes. Imogen saw his high forehead, the swept-back, dark hair. He was, she thought, like the hall they were standing in. Both dark and pale, marble and cool.

Dad pushed the cart to the middle of the hall, leaving a tiny trail of dried grass from its wheels. But Mr Balik didn't seem to notice. In fact, now that there was so much sunlight in the hall, Imogen could see that it was far from clean. There were scatterings of straw in places over the floor and some grey planks of wood leaned against a wall. They looked as if they belonged in some yard. As if they'd been thrown aside a year or more ago and left there.

Mr Balik stood with his feet apart, watching as the first owl was unpacked from its straw and set down for him to see. He made no reaction but Grainger, leaning back on his haunches, let out a soft whistle and looked slowly from Dad to Mr Balik. His face showed the faintest trace of puzzlement.

'Don't stop there, man,' Mr Balik said to him. 'We'll see the lot, if you don't mind.'

'Yes, sir,' said Grainger, but Imogen thought he looked uneasy.

Once or twice, as she lifted a figure carefully out of the cart, she risked a glance at Mr Balik. His eyes moved a little, taking in the details, but his face was set. She couldn't tell what he was thinking.

'What's this?' he said when the last figure was set before him. 'Thirteen?'

'Yes, sir,' said Dad. 'We made an extra. Against something going wrong with the firing.'

'I asked for twelve.'

'Yes . . . I know, Mr Balik. I just thought . . .'

'One's for luck,' said Imogen.

She surprised herself by daring to speak and

immediately wished she'd kept quiet. Mr Balik turned to her.

'Luck? Where does luck come into it? I wanted twelve. I did not want extras. These were to be the only owls of their kind. Didn't you understand that?'

'Of course, sir . . .'

'Then why thirteen, man? Don't you trust your own craft?'

Dad was silenced. He waited, with his head bowed, as Mr Balik dropped on one knee to examine the owls more carefully. Minutes passed in silence. Then:

'What's the matter with this one?'

'Which one?'

'This,' said Mr Balik, standing and catching up one of the figures. 'It's cracked. Here, across its face.'

'What?' said Dad. Alarm made him bold and he took the owl from Mr Balik's hand. Mr Balik released it as if he wanted no more to do with it and Dad fumbled it before bringing it up to his eyes to examine it.

'Perfect, they had to be,' said Mr Balik. 'Twelve perfect owls. Are the others all right?'

He got down on his hands and knees, like some urgent animal, to look at the others.

'The cart took a bump,' mumbled Dad. 'On our way up here.'

But Mr Balik wasn't listening. He took hold of the owls one by one, turning them over and studying them closely. Imogen held her breath but he found nothing wrong with the remaining twelve.

'Right,' he said at last. 'Twelve, as requested.

You can pay for these, Grainger. But that one . . .' He nodded sharply at the thirteenth owl in Dad's hand. 'That I want destroyed. Do you understand me? I don't want anyone else to see it.'

They weren't sure whether to be pleased or disappointed after their encounter with Mr Balik. He had accepted and paid for his twelve owls – and good money, too – but he'd said nothing about liking or admiring them. And Dad was always more pleased by praise for his work than by payment. He was thoughtful and quiet as they trundled the almost empty cart down the hill again. Getting the job and making the owls had, for all his worries, put some edge and excitement into him. There were heavy coins in his pocket but it wasn't the same.

Whatever the outcome, though, it was a relief to be out of that house. Those tall doors, leading to corridors leading to emptiness; they disturbed Imogen.

When they were almost home, they saw a tall man with sandy hair leaning against the shop door. It was Old Carter, waiting to have a word with them.

'Boy tells me you've crowned him one with your hand cart,' he said.

'I would've done,' Dad told him, 'but he was too quick for me.'

'Why, what's to do?'

'He shot out of the snicket by the church like a rat out of a stack, Carter. Rammed straight into the side of a fully loaded cart.'

'I thought it might be something like that. His mother did too, only she said to come and find out.'

'He didn't mean to,' said Imogen. 'He wasn't looking where he was going.'

'He doesn't know where he's going half the time. His Mother said I was to give you a wigging if you were responsible and pass on her apologies if it was down to Boy.'

'Well,' said Dad, 'it's down to Boy all right.'

'Then I'm sorry for it. Did he do you much damage?'

'Very nearly. He all but put me the wrong side of old Balik. There were a dozen pieces survived the blow but . . .'

'But it was all right, really,' cut in Imogen. 'Mr Balik liked the work.'

'Ah,' said Old Carter. 'So you were on your way to the big house, were you? With the pots, was it?'

'That's right. They were owls. How did you know about them?'

'Grainger told me, though he didn't say they were owls. Said the old devil wanted some kind of work off you.'

'Is that so?' said Dad, a little put out that Old Carter should know so much about it. 'Grainger does talk, then? He said precious little to us.'

'He'll talk if you've got time to wait and listen,' said Old Carter. 'In fact he more or less got the jabbers over these blessed pots.'

'Well, I can't think why that should be.'

'Nor me. Still, there's no point trying to work Grainger out after all those years at the big house. He told me that Balik wanted pottery for each of his outward rooms. He intends to stand them on the window ledges.'

'What for?'

'God knows, potter. There's only him and Grainger up there to see them. Still, I haven't the patience to work out the ways of the rich. And I don't suppose you mind what he does with them.'

'Not now he's paid up, I don't.'

Old Carter shuffled back up the road to report his findings to his wife while Dad unlocked the shop. Imogen took the handcart round the back and removed the thirteenth owl. She lifted it delicately from its straw, carried it into the kiln-room and placed it on the bench.

Fortune was a good name for her little owl, she thought. It would make a good name for this one too. Mr Balik didn't like the idea of there being thirteen owls but, if it hadn't been for the extra one, his order couldn't have been met. The twelfth owl would have been damaged and then it was quite likely that he'd have refused the lot.

Dad came through from the yard and stopped in his tracks at the sight of the clay figure on the bench. He snatched up a sack and tossed it over its head.

'Don't cover it,' said Imogen.

'I'm not just covering it up,' he said. 'This is to stop the pieces flying.'

'Why? What are you going to do?'

'What I said I would.' He took up a hammer and tapped the shaft against his palm. 'Destroy it.'

'No,' said Imogen, catching his arm. 'Don't smash it.'

'I promised, Imogen. I have to.'

'Please. Mr Balik said he didn't want anyone to see it. They won't if I keep it in my room, will they?'

'Keep it?' he said, looking at her with a puzzled frown. 'What do you want to keep it for?'

'Because my little owl was smashed and . . . and I want this one to take his place. To remember things by . . .'

'But Imogen, it's not even right. Its face is cracked. You can't want it.'

She wasn't expecting him to say that. She flinched, just a little, and looked steadily at him. He stared back at her for no more than a moment and then lowered his eyes.

'Can't want it?' she said. 'Because its face is cracked?'

'Yes, well . . .'

He placed the hammer gently on the bench and moved towards the door. 'Perhaps you should take it, Imogen,' he said over his shoulder. 'It's mostly your work after all, I suppose. But Mr Balik mustn't know. You mustn't tell anyone.'

He's afraid, thought Imogen for the first time. Afraid of Mr Balik, and of me.

'I won't say anything, Dad,' she said. 'And, anyway, who is there to tell?'

Fortune, the thirteenth owl, stood on the ledge of Imogen's square window. It looked out, over the red-tiled roof of the kiln-room, towards the fields. Imogen lay on her bed and watched it. By moving her head a little from side to side, she made it appear to sway. Gently, as if it was attending to the movement of some field-mouse or vole in the distance.

After a while, she repositioned it so that its eyes were staring into the room. Deep, black holes in its flat face; but, somehow, not empty. The face had a troubled look. It was lit down one side by the low sun and the fine crack across its cheek appeared to glisten. Almost as if it were moist.

'What's the matter?' Imogen said softly. 'Are you sad?'

The owl looked silently into the room.

Eventually Imogen's eyes closed and through the blackness of sleep the sound came back to her – that rattling undertone she'd heard from the kiln. A tangle of shaken wires, a breeze disturbing the leaves of a silver birch.

She tried to drag herself back to wakefulness but she didn't have the strength. The sound hissed around her room, both inside and outside her head. Dream and reality.

6

A block of sunlight came in at the back door and angled over the kitchen table. Imogen's head was resting on the table when the shadow appeared behind her. So sharp and clear that it seemed to be more than shadow, to have a substance of its own. She felt the cold weight of it on her arm. A shape, falling across the kitchen table and moving its head from side to side. It was the size of a tall man but in its precise outline she could see feathers, the hook of a beak glimpsed before the head turned and the outline was lost.

Imogen could not bring herself to look. The shadow grew across the table in front of her. It obliterated the sunlight. She felt something move to stand behind her.

A broad man in a black suit with the head of a bird. A thin skin, laced with red veins, over the swelling of its eyes. It opened its beak, wide and silent.

The sound that filled her ears was Imogen's own shout. She sat up in bed and leaned forward to prop her head on her knees. It was still dark and the house was quiet.

First there had been the rattling sound from the

kiln, as she was falling asleep, then this; a man-bird standing at her back, made blind by skin stretched over its eyes.

Imogen had seen him without turning round. Somehow she'd been high above the kitchen and had seen herself sitting at the table with the man-bird behind her. When she closed her eyes now she could see him again. This time, though, she knew it was only the memory of the dream and not the dream itself. The danger wasn't close. All the same, she climbed out of bed, took her mother's cloak and pulled a chair to the window. She rested her elbows on the ledge, determined to stay awake till she saw the first streaks of light sky above the fields.

The folds of the cloak made a good pillow. She liked the fading grey of it, and its heaviness. It seemed to comfort her and, gradually, the dream began to lose its vividness and slip out of her mind.

The cloak was almost all there was in the house to remind her that once she'd had a mother. Sometimes she stopped to look at the photograph above the fireplace, when Dad wasn't around, but it didn't mean as much to her as the cloak. A lady resting a hand on the back of a chair. Not smiling, rather sombre. Imogen was sure she hadn't been as serious as that. The cloak told a different story. It felt like a plump arm across her shoulders.

There were times when she wanted to ask Dad about her but something in his face always stopped her. Some shadow of loss, perhaps. Her mother had died such a long time ago, even before the accident in the kiln-room, and yet he still couldn't bring himself to talk about her.

Before the dawn came Imogen had fallen asleep.

'Are you all right, Imogen,' Dad asked her in the morning. 'You look a little tired to me.'

'Oh,' she said, 'I had a dream. It woke me up.'

'A bad dream?'

'Just enough to wake me.'

She wanted him to ask more about it but he wouldn't. He was centring clay on the wheel; making himself busy. If he'd asked what her dream was about she might've tried to tell him. Part of her wanted to tell him. If she put it in words for him, said it out loud, it might not have seemed so bad. She might even have been glad to hear him laugh it off.

'Did I wake you?' she asked.

'Wake me?'

'Yes. I think I called out.'

'I didn't hear anything, sweet. You know me. I never wake up, even when I'm supposed to.'

Oh yes, she knew him. She knew when he tried not to look at her because he was fussing over a job he normally did without thinking. When he had things to say but wouldn't open his mouth.

In the evening she went out for a walk and Boy and his dog emerged from nowhere and tagged along. Imogen sighed and said nothing. But she noticed a difference in Boy. There were still sidelong glances at her, making her feel as if she were part of some circus, but there was no mockery in them. Perhaps the bang on his skull had knocked the taunting out of him, she thought.

She'd planned to go down the lane and cut across the fields, like she used to do, but the thought of Boy dragging behind her and yattering nonsense all the way made her change her mind. She turned right and headed up towards the church.

'Your mum's looking for you,' she said.

'What?'

'She's looking out the window. See. I think she wants you.'

'No she don't. She just told me to clear out.'

'Oh. I wonder why?'

'Says I've been under her feet. Ted showed me where there's badgers. D'you want to see?'

'No.'

'It's a bit early, though. They don't come out till it's getting dark. You seen old Balik lately?'

'We took the cart up there the other day. Remember?'

'That man's a bastard. A right bastard.'

'You shouldn't say things like that, Boy.'

'He is, though. I heard my Dad say so. He's a right old bastard, he said.'

'You just like saying the word.'

'I don't.'

Imogen didn't argue. If I don't say anything, she thought, he might go away.

'A right, proper old bastard.' Boy muttered darkly. 'Bloody old bastard of a bastard. I hate him. You know what he's done now?'

'What?'

'He told off Ted and his brother to their old man.'

In spite of herself Imogen wanted to hear more about Mr Balik.

'What for?' she asked.

'For poking around his garden.'

'Well, they shouldn't have been there, should they?'

'Didn't do him no harm, though. And it's bloody big enough. It weren't nothing to get stewed up about. What was they doing anyway? Squashing his precious grass flat?'

'It was trespass, though.'

'Oo-er. Tresp-arse.'

'They asked for it, Boy.'

'Asked for it? For him to come flying out and give them both a cut of the lug? Then tell their old man so's he can give them a leathering? Bastard.'

'I'll tell your mum what you say.'

'You won't. You'll have to say it yourself. Then you'll be in trouble.'

'You wait and see, then.'

Boy fell silent for a while. By this time they'd reached the church. Imogen thought about going into the yard but she didn't like the idea of Boy, with his foul mouth and his scruffy dog, following her. So she walked on, out of the village.

In a little while they came to Mr Balik's drive, as she knew they would. She wanted to stop and turn round before they reached it but she couldn't do that without giving Boy a reason. And Boy would nag her for a reason and not be fobbed off with anything that sounded weak or vague.

An iron gate, permanently open and overgrown between two tall pillars marked the entrance. She hesitated outside, looking up the drive. It was overhung with trees, almost like a tunnel, and curved away to the right, up to the big house. The house itself couldn't be seen from the road.

As they stood there, the dog started to whimper. It crouched down on its haunches and rolled its eyes at Boy.

'He wants to run,' said Imogen. 'Why don't you take him into the fields?'

'No. Someone's coming. Listen.'

He dropped to his knees and wrapped his arms around the dog's neck. The jingle of harness came to them through the trees.

'It's Balik,' said Boy.

He picked up the dog and wrestled it into the bushes by one of the pillars. It writhed in his grasp and its whimpering became more urgent.

'Quiet, you daft thing!' hissed Boy, and clamped his hands round the dog's jaws.

Imogen waited. Why should she hide from Mr Balik? She'd done nothing. And she was on the public highway, not his property. Then she heard Mr Balik shout something at his horse, sounding very close. She glanced up and saw a blur of high-trotting front legs, the mass of the horse's neck, twisted and pulled back. And the toe of Mr Balik's boot.

Immediately she shook herself into movement and ran for safety, throwing herself down next to Boy. Her face was pressed into the turf but she didn't dare to move. She held her breath and listened to the thud of the horse's feet pass by.

'He's gone,' said Boy eventually. 'Down the lane and into the village.'

'Why'd you hide like that?' Imogen asked sharply. 'There was no need.'

'Why'd you do it, then?'

She stood up and swiped at the few wet leaves clinging to her dress. Then she looked down at Boy fiercely, as if she might take a swing at him. He remained crouched in the grass. The dog was trying to twist its head free from his grip. He struggled to hold on but it gave a sudden jerk and spilled out of his arms.

'All right, all right,' he said. 'You don't like him either, do you, boy?'

The dog backed away, lowering itself to the ground and yapping.

'No,' said Imogen. 'It's not that. It's not Mr Balik he doesn't like . . .'

''Course it is. Look at him.'

It yapped once more and then sprinted off down the lane, the same way that Mr Balik had gone.

'He's frightened of the place,' said Imogen quietly, not really for Boy to hear. 'He can't abide being near this place.'

Boy jumped up and took off after his dog. His squeaky shouts faded quickly among the trees.

'Come back here! You hear me! Come back, you bastard!'

The sight of Boy's dog, struggling and whimpering outside the gate, kept coming back to Imogen. She wondered whether it had some memory of the place. Perhaps Mr Balik or Grainger had found it sniffing around up there and had chased it off. She could imagine Mr Balik giving the poor creature the toe of his boot. Maybe it was as simple as that, a hazy memory of being frightened.

She didn't think so, though. The more she thought about it, the more it seemed as if the dog had seen something, something that was hidden from everyone else. Some unreal thing, like a figure in a dream.

And Imogen knew what dreams could be like.

On some nights she saw nothing and was only aware of that rattling sound, and sensed unseen things swooping in the black air above her. At other times her dreams were astonishing and vivid; a great wall of fire, sucked towards her down a picture-lined corridor; tiny figures dancing from side to side inside the flames; or the man-bird, also coming towards her, staring at her out of its skin-covered, unseeing eyes. It never made any sound but gaped its beak wide as if it intended to.

When she woke from these dreams, she paced barefoot around her room, or took her chair to the window to wait until morning. She comforted herself by touching the cool flank of Fortune, stroking him gently. He kept her company, looking into the room while she looked out. Once she thought she heard Dad stirring in his room in the loft and seemed to see a thin bar of candlelight under her door. She waited for a knock but none came.

One night, after about a week of this, Imogen woke and didn't know where she was. There was a patch of pale blue light on the floor, in a pattern of twisted squares, and she could feel the roughness of scuffed wood under her fingers. Out of place but familiar. She was in the shop, she realized slowly. Stretched out on the floor, her fingers like claws, her body stiff and arched and her head bent backwards as she stared out of the window at the moon.

In a moment her body relaxed and she felt the world righting itself, becoming ordinary again. And here she was, on the floor of her father's shop, small and foolish. Her head was spinning and she choked, suddenly and loudly, with frustration. She rolled over and sobbed. Her tears soaked into the pale floorboards.

The air was still and heavy and when she got back to her room she opened the window. Then she stretched out on her bed, very weak, and closed her eyes. Immediately she saw the man with the bird head. Standing over the bed like a doctor. But when she opened her eyes she saw nothing.

Not a dream, she thought. I'm wide awake. And there's a sound – a sound in the room.

It was a sound that didn't belong. The hard rustling of plates or tiles settling. Over by the window. Fortune on the ledge, hunched to take off. Moving. Stepping to one side. Stepping back. And rattling his wing tips against the glass.

Imogen sat up slowly. Then, as she was standing, she saw the owl spring.

'No,' she whispered. 'Don't go.'

But Fortune disappeared into shadow and the window ledge was empty, nothing but space. She ran across the room and looked out. The moon, high above a layer of silver cloud, looked bigger from up here. For a moment she remained at the window, feeling as if the emptiness was passing into her body. Then she saw him, perched on the low roof of the kiln-room. And she knew he was waiting for her.

She snatched up the faded grey cloak and padded downstairs again, carrying her boots so she shouldn't wake Dad. As soon as she opened the back door to the night, Fortune lifted from the roof and swooped away again. Over the top of the shop, in the direction of the street. She struggled into the boots and ran round to the street. Almost at once she caught sight of him again, sitting on the thatch of Old Carter's cottage.

She followed him, from roof to chimney stack, from pub sign to fence post, up the street. Fortune kept ahead of her, stopping to wait for her, swaying from side to side, looking at her from his cracked face. And each time he landed it was easy to find him because Imogen knew where he was heading.

Mr Balik's house. Mr Balik himself must've been in there, perhaps awake, pacing up and down, but great as her fear of him was it was not as strong as her urge to follow Fortune wherever he led her. To a window on the ground floor. It was wide open, as if ready for her. She stood beneath it, smelling dew-damp earth and rich, sweet flowers from a nearby bed. The room before her was full of squares and shadows. She saw the sheen of a long table and little else that had a proper shape. Close to her on the window ledge stood a pottery owl but it wasn't Fortune. He was in the room somewhere. She couldn't see him but she sensed it. She stood quite still, not knowing what to do now that she was here.

Then she heard the sharp scrape of metal against brick. Another window being opened. Above her head, on the first floor. She looked up and saw the flicker of candle light and a dark arm holding the window catch. She shrank back against the wall.

'Who is it?' said Mr Balik. 'Who's there?'

His voice was soft but it filled the night. There was no other sound. Imogen saw him lean out of the window. The pale oval of his face against solid blackness as he turned his head slowly, searching the grounds. Her arms and legs began to shake but she stayed where she was, waiting for him to withdraw. Down in the village the church clock began to strike the hour. Before the last chime of two o'clock had faded away, she heard another sound. Inside the ground floor room this time. A rattle and a hiss. And there was a shape swooping at her out of the shadows. Fortune, flying at the open window.

Imogen fell back against the wall and cried out as the thirteenth owl passed over her head, dipped low against the ground and disappeared.

'I see you!' Mr Balik shouted down at her. 'What do you think you're playing at?'

She picked herself up and ran. Straight away from the house, towards the cover of the shadowy trees, her cloak billowing behind her. Mr Balik cursed loudly but she couldn't make out the words. Just angry shouting. Then he stopped. She imagined that he was hurrying through the house, clattering down the staircase or flinging open a cabinet to get to a gun.

At the head of the drive, gasping for breath, she stopped and looked back. No. He was still at the window. Standing there in silence. No more than a shadow in the weak light of the candle. Looking straight at her through the darkness.

Then he shouted again. One long cry, as if he'd been stabbed, but very clear.

'Charlotte!'

7

'You're up late,' Dad said.

There was no lightness in his voice. He wanted to know the reason, suspected he wouldn't like it, but still didn't ask. Didn't even turn round to look at her.

'I was tired,' she told him from the door of the shop. 'I've been walking a lot.'

She hadn't been walking but he wouldn't know that. Or, if he did, he wouldn't say so. She came and stood beside him. He was packing two large plates in a canvas bag.

'These are to go up to the church,' he said. 'Will they be safe in this bag, do you think?'

Imogen didn't answer. Her limbs felt stiff and last night's fear was still inside her. When she'd got home she'd found Fortune back on the window ledge. Cold and still but looking at her as if he wondered where she'd been. Almost disapproving. She'd felt like smashing him. Picking him up in both hands and bringing his head down on the ledge. She'd leaned against her door, picturing this. Hearing the sound. Seeing the fragments scatter over the floor. Then she'd fallen into bed and slept.

'I'll take them if you like,' she said to Dad. It suddenly seemed a good idea to go up to the church.

'All right. But don't take them to the vicarage. Leave them on the old oak chest by the font. The vicar won't want to be disturbed.'

The plates weren't heavy but Imogen packed the bag into the handcart to be sure she wouldn't drop them. She walked steadily up the hill, keeping to the middle of the street where there were fewer ruts.

Sharp memories of last night kept coming to her. Fortune gliding out of the open window. Mr Balik's face in the light of the candle. That name, shouted after her as she ran away. But they didn't come in any sensible sequence. They were like shards, pieces that might make a proper shape if she could put them together. And they were muddled with quite ordinary thoughts.

She found herself wondering where Boy Carter was, whether he was lurking round some corner, waiting with more silly things to tell her. She hadn't bothered to make sure the coast was clear before setting out. And it was too late now. If Boy was watching her somewhere he didn't show himself. Still, she was glad to reach the safety of the churchyard and carry the plates through the heavy oak doors into that cool gloom. She preferred the church when it was empty. On Sunday mornings the pews were full of neighbours looking out of the corners of their eyes and worrying about the tightness of their collars and the neatness of their boots. A stiff, uneasy place on a Sunday.

She took the plates to the black chest by the font and spent some moments arranging them so that the vicar would notice them when he came in and be pleased with them. Then she sat in one of the pews and looked up at the wooden roof boards, so high above her with so much cool air floating in between. She was grateful for that centuries old peace. It made her feel safe.

Then there was a clank at the door.

Imogen sank lower in her pew, conscious that she was sitting where she shouldn't be. Footsteps clicked over the stone floor. And another sound, too. The light tap of a stick. Each sound seemed large and solemn, rising slowly to lose itself in the air of the nave. A figure passed down the aisle; went beyond her place without noticing her. She knew it was Mr Balik, almost before she saw him out of the corner of her eye.

He walked as far as the altar steps and stopped. One foot on the step, his head bowed. Mr Balik didn't come to the church on Sundays. He was notable by his absence, the villagers said. Imogen watched him standing there uncertainly, both hands pressing on his bent knee. Even from the back he looked uncomfortable, as if all the muscles in his shoulders were tensed.

Suddenly, he drew in a long, loud breath and walked briskly back down the aisle. Then, turning his face briefly in her direction, he noticed Imogen. She saw the moment of recognition in his eyes but it was nothing to do with what he'd seen, or thought he'd seen, last night. Yes, the potter's girl; that cracked little thing. That was all. She stood up slowly and looked at him.

'What are you doing in here?' he said, his voice jarring and loud in the silence of the church.

'I've brought some plates. For the vicar.'

He took a slow step towards her. Against the deep colours of the church window his face looked white as stone.

'Tell me . . .' he began and then stopped, looking at her for several moments, like someone emerging from a dream. Almost helpless.

'What?' asked Imogen.

But he shook his head and didn't answer. Then he turned away and walked quickly out of the church.

Over the next two nights the dream returned. But they remained dreams. Fortune did not move again or call her to follow him.

'And I wouldn't go if he did,' she said to herself. 'I shan't go up there again. Ever.'

One morning, she was sitting in the shop, waiting to open and nodding over a book, when a large cart pulled up outside. The cart was familiar enough; it belonged to Mr Robinson who farmed the bit of land north of the village, beyond the big house. But it was unusual to see it stop at the potter's shop. More so to see Mr Robinson himself swing out of it and clump up to the shop front. He shaded his eyes and pressed his nose against the window. When he caught sight of Imogen, he began to work the handle up and down, very deliberately, and mouth words at her through the glass. Imogen tossed the book down and skipped over to unlock.

'We're not open yet, you know,' she said, holding the door so he couldn't pass. 'What's up?'

'You're ready, are you?' Robinson said.

'Ready for what?'

'You're coming with me, aren't you? To Melling?'

'I don't think I am.'

Dad hurried into the shop from the back and took the door from Imogen. Mr Robinson flexed his neck and shoulder muscles and glanced at Imogen as he stepped inside.

'You're early, Basil,' Dad said.

'This is morning, isn't it?' said Mr Robinson. 'I told you I'd be round in the morning.'

'She'll be with you before too long, Basil. I must have a word first, though.'

'It'll have to be a quick one, mind. I'll be starting when I start, ready or not.'

He marched out of the shop and clambered back on to the cart. Taking a watch from his waistcoat pocket, he glanced from it to Dad who was still standing at the door. Then he began to fill his pipe, again very deliberately. Dad shut the door and turned round to find Imogen staring at him. He knew she would be.

'We're going somewhere?' she said. 'You never said.'

'No, I know. I've been looking for the moment to tell you, sweet.'

'To Melling, he said. What for?'

'To see Helen.'

'Why should you need to find a moment to tell me that?'

'It's been a long time since you've seen your Aunt Helen, Imogen. I thought it would be nice for you . . .'

'What's so hard about telling me, though?'

'The air's so good there. By the sea and everything. So they all say and . . .'

'Dad.'

'Look, Imogen, you need to get away for a spell. I don't think you've been at all right these last few days.'

'I've been as right as anything. I've done all my jobs, haven't I? I haven't been letting you down, have I?'

'Of course you haven't.'

'What is it, then?'

For the first time since he'd come into the shop he lifted his face and looked straight at her. There was a film of moisture on his brow.

'You've not slept at all well, sweet, you know you haven't. Shouting and things. I reckon you need a change. It's not been easy to mention.'

'You mentioned it to Mr Robinson. Why couldn't you talk to me?'

'I just didn't. I just did what I thought best. And I've said nothing to Basil, bar that I want him to take you.'

'To take me? Aren't you coming?'

'I can't leave the work, Imogen. Not now. We've just done that job for Mr Balik and we might get others from it . . .'

'You're sending me away.'

'It's not like that at all. I've done this to help you. Don't look at me like that, Imogen.'

Then she ran out of the shop and up to her room. Cursing him and biting her lip. A small brown case had been placed open on her chair. Her best blouse, the one Dad liked, with the wild roses on it, was draped half-heartedly over the end of the bed. He couldn't even pack properly. She slammed the door shut and, without thinking, began to fling some things into the case. The blouse she left where Dad had put it.

She took the case downstairs and threw it into the back of Mr Robinson's cart. She climbed up beside the farmer, her eyes fixed on the church spire at the top of the street. Mr Robinson flipped the reins, clicked at his horse and they moved off.

'It'll be nice, Imogen,' came her father's voice behind them. 'Helen will spoil you.'

She didn't answer, didn't even turn round.

'You're the wrong side of your Daddy this morning,' mumbled Mr Robinson, half to himself. 'I can tell that much.'

When they pulled past the church and left the last cottages behind, warm tears were running down her cheeks. She shifted herself sideways so that Mr Robinson wouldn't know.

8

When she woke, Imogen wasn't sure where she was. She wondered whether she'd gone downstairs again and was in the shop; but it didn't feel at all like that. There wasn't the touch of floorboards. And she was in a bed. She opened her eyes and looked towards the light. There were rooftops outside. This house was much taller than home. And at the window edge there were bricks, not stone. Aunt Helen's house. She saw on the ceiling the even glow of a sea-sky and thought she could detect the breathing of the sea itself somewhere in the distance.

There were fragments of pictures in her head – pieces of dream left over from the night – but none of them was very clear. It was as if she'd been watching them through some kind of billowing curtain. Whatever they were, though, was nothing to do with the old dreams. There were no thin, dancing creatures in walls of flame, no sightless man-bird.

My memories being washed clean, she thought.

She closed her eyes again and, for several moments, forced the old images to return. It wasn't difficult; they hadn't really gone away. It was as if they were just out of sight somewhere, waiting.

When she went downstairs to breakfast, Aunt Helen was bustling in and out of the kitchen.

'Here she is,' she said, smiling suddenly and folding her hands under her bosom. 'Here's my girl.'

Aunt Helen was a small, talkative woman – not at all like Dad – and she had a way of looking directly at people that reminded Imogen of a robin, hopping around by a gardener's spade. Dad always said that she had more than her fair share of the family talk, and it was true. He'd been left with mumbles and moans and the odd sideways comment.

'I don't know why you want to be up so early, Imogen,' she said. 'You're here to rest, you know. You can stay in bed as long as you like. I don't suppose you get much chance to do that most days, do you?'

She hurried back into the kitchen and Imogen sat down at the table. She noticed with a start that Uncle Jack was also sitting there, leaning forward and sipping carefully from a large mug of tea. He gave her a nod of greeting and looked straight down at his breakfast.

'Imogen's come down, Jack,' came Aunt Helen's voice from the kitchen. 'In case you haven't noticed.'

He smiled and gave Imogen another nod. He looked as if he was about to say something but Aunt Helen appeared in the doorway with a jug of milk.

'Don't mind him, sweetheart. He doesn't mean to be rude. The king himself wouldn't get a word out of Jack before nine in the morning, would he, Jack?'

Jack wiped his moustache between his thumb and finger and raised his eyebrows as if he would answer. But Aunt Helen launched straight into a story about Hobnails, the man who brought the milk.

'He's got it into his head that he has to have a bicycle,' she said. 'To deliver the milk. Well, I explained the nonsense of that to him but you could see he'd already buttoned his ears to any kind of sense. He was the same when he was a kid. Full of far-fetched dreaming but about as quick off the mark as a bullock.'

'Hm . . . hmm . . . uh-huh,' said Jack, nodding and tapping his fork absently on one of Dad's best plates, and gazing through the lace half-curtains as he chewed.

Even when Helen bustled out to the scullery and her voice faded to nothing, the nodding continued. Eventually he swung his coat off the back of the chair and went off to his work down at Melling quay. He winked at Imogen on his way out, though she wasn't sure whether this meant 'goodbye' or 'just listen to your aunt rambling on out there'.

At the end of breakfast Imogen carried the plates out to the kitchen to help with the washing-up but Aunt Helen wouldn't let her do anything.

'No,' she said. 'You're to rest, my girl. And you mustn't put me in trouble with that brother of mine by flitting about all day and every day, finding things to do. If you weren't here I'd have to do things myself so don't you soften me up with help.'

It made Imogen wonder what Dad *had* said to

her. Very little, probably. A few hints about being tired and growing up. Then he'd hope that Helen would somehow guess the rest. Imogen certainly couldn't tell from the way her aunt treated her whether she knew anything more or not. She treated everyone the same; people to talk to or specks of dust to flick out of the way while she bustled about the house.

For a long time Imogen had nothing to do but sit around the house, listening to her aunt talking and occasionally getting in the way.

'You're in my dust, Imogen,' she'd say, swiping at the floor with a broom. 'Why don't you sit down somewhere and rest?'

So she took herself off and sat in the kitchen. She stared out at the little back garden for ages, trying to remember things in their proper order, while Aunt Helen swept the stairs and sang a hymn in the background.

The way she'd followed the thirteenth owl up to Mr Balik's house. Why had she done this? She pictured herself doing it, and now it seemed such a foolish and unthinking thing to have done. Then Fortune flying over her head and across the grass to the trees. Not a real owl. She must've imagined that. Fortune had stayed on her window ledge at home. He must've done. She'd been sleepwalking. Like finding herself downstairs in the shop and not knowing how she came to be there.

But Mr Balik, appearing in the candle light at the upper window, that was real enough. And shouting out so strangely, Charlotte. There was no mistake. He'd called that name.

Aunt Helen backed into the kitchen with her

broom and Imogen almost turned to her and said, 'Who's Charlotte?'

But, of course, Aunt Helen wouldn't have known anything about it.

After a day or two of resting, Imogen decided that she wanted to go down to the sea. There was some vague memory of it from the last time she'd been to visit Aunt Helen. But she'd been so much smaller then. She thought that it might seem different now. More important, somehow; she wasn't sure how. On several occasions she'd walked around Melling and glimpsed it between buildings. And once she'd even ventured briefly on to the quay with its odd mix of salty air and heavy machinery. But Aunt Helen wasn't happy about her straying too far from home.

'There's nothing down there,' she said. 'Only the grain store and you won't be interested in that.'

'Isn't there anything else at all?' asked Imogen.

'Can't you remember?'

'I was only little the last time I was here.'

'Well, there's boats, which aren't interesting either. And The Anchor, which is. Only The Anchor's a sin hole, Imogen. All Christian souls give it a wide berth.'

'Why?'

'Don't ask. Just make sure you never go anywhere near it.'

'What about the sea, though? Couldn't I get a proper look at the sea?'

'You don't want to do that,' said Aunt Helen. 'That's not entirely safe if you haven't got your strength back.'

As if some watery arm would pull her into the waves.

'I have got my strength back, Aunt Helen. And I can't come to any harm by just walking.'

'You let me be the judge of that.'

Eventually, though, towards the end of the week, she agreed that a gentle stroll might be all right.

'You must take it easy, though, Imogen,' Aunt Helen said.

Except when she passed The Anchor, of course. Then she was allowed to hurry.

So Imogen walked slowly down to the quay.

The grain store was a green tower of wood and corrugated iron. She stood beneath it and looked up. A kind of covered bridge reached out across the path and ended high above the hold of an old coaster. Aunt Helen was wrong about the boats. Imogen found this one fascinating. It sat impossibly in the water, so heavy and solid.

She passed under the bridge, and caught sight of The Anchor a little way along the quay. A squat little pub with thick white walls, its weathered door shut tight. Full of old men playing dominoes, Imogen thought. Not nearly as interesting as the coaster. Although Aunt Helen would probably consider dominoes a danger to the soul.

She reached the stone steps which led to the beach and then trod steadily along the soft sand, keeping her head down. She didn't want to take in the sweep of the sea until she'd left the town far behind her. When at last she stopped, she sat down where the rough grass had made the sand more firm, and looked out, quite deliberately, across the North Sea.

She couldn't remember seeing anything so big. Or empty.

She narrowed her eyes but couldn't tell where sky began and water ended. The sky was a shining pearl grey. The darker grey of the sea came lapping towards her in endless lines of little waves. They ran in, building as if they'd break, and then folding over and falling in on themselves. Sliding back tamely under the mass of waiting sea. Purring and hissing, amounting to nothing. Again and again.

A small boat with an orange sail was moving slowly across the bay. Imogen watched it until it rounded the headland and disappeared. Then she noticed that two or three bright stars had appeared above the layers of pink-grey clouds.

She stood stiffly and began the walk back towards the quay. The little town was showing several golden lights at windows and the land behind it was soft with darkness. It all looked so safe, she thought, and predictable.

Crunching up the damp steps from the beach, she began to walk back along the path in the direction of the grain store. It was about a quarter of a mile away, she guessed. The bulk of the coaster was still resting against the quay, its lights now trembling on the still water. Some men were swinging ropes and busying themselves with the shoot for the last loading of the day. Flecks floated in the yellow light which spilled from the store. The men were calling to each other with faint voices. Such activity, she thought. Everyone busy with his own job, knowing exactly what to do.

As she passed The Anchor the door burst open and made her jump. She heard the wheeze of an accordion inside, and laughter. She slowed a little and, without quite turning her head, looked in. But she saw almost nothing because, at that moment, two men ducked out of the door and blocked her view. They leaned, dark against the white-washed wall, and she felt their eyes pick her out and follow her. One of them mumbled something and the other laughed. She quickened her step, hurrying towards the activity and noise ahead.

She stopped, a little breathlessly, by the bow of the coaster. Its flank was streaked with rust and coils of grimy rope, as thick as a man's arm, were strewn on its foredeck. She breathed the heavy air, a mixture of engine oil and the clean dry smell of the grain.

The scratch of a boot on cobbles made her turn round. A man was standing a few yards away, facing her in the shadow of the grain store. One of the men from The Anchor. Her heart began to thump and she looked round wildly.

There were three men on the boat. Two were holding the shoot as the last dribbles of grain fell into the hold. The other sat on a box smoking a pipe. He had his back to her. She thought of calling out to him but didn't know what to say. High above her a fourth man was perched in the opening, silhouetted in the square of warm light.

She looked back the way she'd come. No safety there. Only The Anchor with its cheery music, and, in the distance, the steps down to the empty beach. On the other side of the grain store was the alleyway which led up to the town. But that was dark too, and she'd have to pass close to the man in the shadow to reach it.

Imogen took a step towards him.
'Miss?' he said softly.
If he moved she would push him as hard as she could and then run. He swayed, a half motion in her direction, and at the same time there was a shout from above. She looked up and pushed in one movement. Her hands felt the rough material of the man's smock for a brief moment. Then he was stumbling backwards, away from her. And out of the sky something was swooping down at them. A solid black shape, coming down like a striking bird. It brushed the man's smock and cracked on to the cobbles between them. Sparks jagged off the stone.
The man groaned quietly and tried to sit up. Then fell back again and lay still. Imogen sank to her knees and sat down in the road.
There was a pulse of silence before she heard the sailors from the boat running towards them. An orange lamp was swinging through the darkness. When it settled it made a pool of light on the road. Imogen saw the knees and hands of the men and one or two moon-like faces. One of them, she noted without surprise, belonged to Uncle Jack. In the middle of the pool of light, by the fallen man's feet, was a block and tackle, blue-black metal with a thick hook, the size of a small gravestone.
'You all right?' someone said.
There was no answer. Another voice added in a whisper, 'He's like a sheet but he's still breathing. Not a mark on him.'
'It missed the beggar,' said the first voice, 'by a whisker.'
The lamp was held over the man's head. He was blinking and moving his mouth. His face, bright on

one side, in shadow on the other, looked puzzled. At the sight of him Imogen caught her breath and the men looked round, taking her in for the first time.

'My God, it's a girl.'

Black shining eyes and a peppery beard loomed out of the darkness at her.

'That's right,' said Uncle Jack, flat and matter-of-fact. 'It's my niece.'

'And who the hell's this character?' said the bearded sailor, turning to the man at their feet.

'I think I know him,' said Imogen quietly.

And she looked again to make sure.

'Yes,' she said. 'His name's Grainger.'

Aunt Helen enjoyed the fuss. The bearded sailor and Uncle Jack helped Grainger into the high-backed chair in the front room. She skipped ahead of them to whisk the cover off it and then darted out to boil the kettle.

'I'm all right,' Grainger told the men testily. 'A bit done in, that's all. I didn't know where I was.'

'You bloody near had your head caved in,' said the sailor. 'If this lass hadn't shoved you . . . well, I don't like to think.'

Imogen was standing by the door, still holding on to the handle. Grainger wiped his mouth and looked at her. His skin was the colour of a candle.

'It is you,' he said. 'The potter's child.'

Uncle Jack was twisting a leather cap in his hands. He looked almost as numbed as Grainger.

'That block and tackle,' he mumbled. 'I did say it weren't right. I did say it should've been looked at.'

The sailor slapped him across the shoulder.
'Come you on,' he said. 'The bloke's in one piece so don't fret about it. I'm off to have a drink,' he added with a wink at Grainger. 'To your health.' Then he pushed his way out of the room.

'I should see what Helen's up to,' said Uncle Jack, and he shrank out of the room.

'I'll come with you,' Imogen added quickly.

'No. Wait.'

Grainger was leaning forward in Aunt Helen's chair, his elbows on his knees, looking down at his feet.

'You was very quick,' he said. 'Like lightning. I reckon I must say thank you.'

'I wasn't that quick. I didn't really see . . .'

'What?'

'Nothing.'

'I'd've been dead. Half an hour back and I could've been a dead man.'

'You were . . . watching me.'

'Yes.'

'I saw you come out of The Anchor.'

'I was watching you. At first I just looks up and sees a pretty girl.'

Because it was dark, she thought. And probably the drink.

'Then I thinks I know who that is.'

He spoke carefully, like a man not used to words.

'I seen you before,' he went on. 'So I went along to see if I was right. And . . . well, the bloody sky come down on me.'

He was grinning down at his boots. A brief, inward grin. It was the first time she'd seen him look other than impassive. And at that point Aunt Helen hurried in with the teapot.

'Jack,' she called over her shoulder, 'go you upstairs and fetch a blanket. No, no,' she added to Grainger. 'Don't you get up. Stay where you are. You've got a touch of the shocks and you'll have to watch that.'

She put the teapot on the hearth and pulled up a stool so she could sit by Grainger's feet.

'Now. I want to know exactly what happened, start to finish. It's no good asking Jack. He puts everything into one sentence. Move yourself in, Imogen. You'll have to do some of the poor man's talking for him.'

The following morning Aunt Helen told Imogen to walk down to The Anchor with some fruit loaf for Mr Grainger.

'Don't go in,' she said. 'Just tap at the door. And you can tell him he doesn't have to stay there. I don't know how anyone could sleep in a place like that. What with all those daft old boys hawking and spitting in the bar all night. There's a bed up here if he wants it.'

'He's not hurt,' said Imogen. 'And I think he likes to keep to himself.'

'That's just what I'm telling you. He's not by himself with half the drinking population of the town beneath his feet, is he? And anyway, he's Mr Balik's man. It's a family connection. In a manner of speaking.'

Imogen said nothing but wrapped the fruit loaf in a cloth and set off for The Anchor. She was still unsure of Grainger and had no intention of inviting him back to the house. Besides, it annoyed her to see Aunt Helen make such a stir over him. As if he were royalty or something. And not because of any grandness in Grainger himself but because of the link with Mr Balik.

You wouldn't fuss over Mr Balik if you knew what I knew, she thought. If you'd seen him lay into Boy Carter for no good reason and stalk through the village like a thunder cloud. And everybody hating the sight of him.

But, as far as Aunt Helen was concerned, Mr Balik was one of the masters. You had to be proud to walk the same path as the likes of him. And if you couldn't pander to the master himself, you pandered to his man.

The front door of The Anchor was shut when she got there and Imogen knocked lightly, hoping no one would come. She was wondering whether to leave the loaf by the foot-scraper when the door opened and Grainger came out.

'Oh,' he said. 'Was you knocking?'

'Yes. I brought this. From Aunt Helen.'

'Right,' said Grainger. He took it awkwardly and, after a moment's uncertainty, turning it over in his large hands, he carried it into the pub. She was left on the pavement, not sure whether he intended to come out again or not.

'Tell her thank you,' he said, re-emerging.

'It's a fruit loaf,' said Imogen. In case you were wondering, she thought.

'Oh.' There was a long pause. 'Look, I'm off back to the village tomorrow. I only come with a load of Balik's grain. That's why I'm here. He won't come here himself, you see.'

He looked as if he wanted Imogen to say something but she didn't. He cleared his throat and set off across the road. Then hesitated. To see if she would follow, Imogen thought. The tide was out and several silvery banks of sand had appeared where yesterday there had only been sea. He looked out of place, standing there with this expanse of beach and water at his back.

'Well,' Imogen called over to him, 'I suppose I must . . .'

'Them owls,' he said suddenly. And stopped.

Imogen took a breath and crossed the road after him. They began to walk along the quay in the direction of the beach.

'What about them?'

'You brought them up to the house, didn't you? You and your old man?'

'Yes.'

'He did the deal but I heard that it was you actually made them. Was that right?'

'I made the first one.'

'What was it behind them, then?'

'Behind them?'

'Why did it have to be owls?'

She wasn't sure that she should tell him. She hadn't told anyone else so why should she say anything to this straight-backed, silent man?

'There's something about them, isn't there?' he went on. 'Something a bit funny, if you see what I mean.'

Standing there, so far from home and in such odd circumstances, was like being in another country. On the edge of some desert, perhaps, where ordinary life had somehow stopped. Maybe things were so strange here, she thought, that it would be possible to say something to Grainger. Maybe she could try and see what happened.

'It was when you burnt the old barn down,' she said. 'You and Mr Balik.'

'Ah, yes. I remember that. You came charging down over the field. Shouting at us. Was that something to do with it?'

'I saw an owl in that barn, yes.'

'Burned, was it?' he said, pausing to stare out at the sea.

'I don't know. I thought it might be. That's why I made the model. I made a little model out of a bit of clay. The others were copied from that.'

'Yes?'

'Mr Balik saw it – the model, I mean – and he told us to make some more. Life size . . .'

'Which I know about, yes.'

He carried on walking for a while in silence. Climbed down the stone steps to the beach. Arms swinging steadily by his side, as if he had somewhere special to go.

'I don't know why he wanted them,' said Imogen after some minutes.

'You don't?'

'I suppose he just liked the model.'

'I suppose so. Except . . .'

'What?'

'Can you meet me by the road into Melling this afternoon? Near the Cottage Hospital?'

'What for?'

'I want to show you something. Do you know where I mean?'

'Yes, I think so.'

'I'll wait there at two o'clock. Come if you can.'

They stopped walking and faced the sea. Imogen squinted back at the huddle of buildings far behind them on the quay. She waited for Grainger to say something else but he remained silent. For several moments she watched a scattering of little birds with stick legs run about at the edge of the water.

'Two o'clock, then,' he said, turning back. 'If you can make it.'

Aunt Helen wanted to know how Grainger was looking, what he said and whether he was pleased about the loaf.

'He was very grateful,' Imogen told her. She couldn't remember him saying anything at all about the loaf but it didn't feel much like a lie to pretend he had. He probably was grateful. She thought he wasn't used to receiving gifts.

'So what did he have to say for himself?'

'Not much. Hardly anything, really.'

'Well, Imogen, you've been gone nearly the full hour. He must've said something.'

Aunt Helen found it impossible to think of two people spending so long together without indulging in full and wide-ranging conversation. 'Hardly anything' merely fired her curiosity.

'You didn't set foot inside that place, I hope,' she said.

'No, Aunt Helen. I knocked and waited for him to come out.'

'And he's recovered from his mishap?'

'Yes. He's back to normal.'

'Except that he's lost his powers of speech apparently.'

'Well, he never did have much to say for himself.'

'Huh. You and I know too many men like that, Imogen. Nothing to say for themselves because there's not much in their heads, I suppose. Perhaps he'd've been better off if he *did* get a crash on the skull.'

After lunch Imogen asked her if she could go out again. Just for a walk, to get some exercise.

'You can shake the rugs with me. There's plenty of exercise in that.'

'I could do that later. I thought I'd just wander round. See the place while I've still got the chance.'

'See Melling? What is there to see? I'd've thought you'd had enough of the quayside to last a lifetime.'

'Somewhere else, then. Away from the sea.'

'All right. If you must. But I won't be saving the rugs up for you. They'll have to be done when I'm ready.'

Until then Imogen hadn't been sure that it would be right to meet Grainger again. He wasn't the easiest person to be with. But she said she wanted to go out and now she found that she really was anxious to hear more about Mr Balik. Something to do with the owls and with Melling itself. She avoided mentioning any of this to Aunt Helen and that didn't feel much like a lie either. As she walked up the hill to the edge of town, though, she began to feel uncertain about it. She would have liked her aunt's approval for this meeting.

Just after two she found Grainger sitting on a hump of grass at the crossroads by the Melling sign. He stood up when he saw her and nodded, as if in answer to a question.

'It's further up the hill here,' he said and, just as

he'd done in the morning, walked away from her. She hurried to catch him and walked by his side, not too close.

'I come here two or three times in the year,' he said after a while. 'But like I said, Balik never does. It's several years since he came to Melling.'

'Why doesn't he come here?' Imogen asked. Only for something to say. She didn't see why Mr Balik should want to come to Melling anyway.

'This is what I'm going to show you. Look up there, beyond that hedge.'

She saw the grey roof of a large house between tree-tops.

'The house? What is it?'

'It's not my business to tell you this. Balik ain't never said don't; but I know he wouldn't want me to. Only, there was a lady lived in that house once.'

'Lady?' said Imogen quickly.

'A long time ago, before he ever came to the village. Did you ever hear about that?'

'No,' she said. 'Never.'

'Oh. Only people do talk in the village.'

'Not to me. I mean, not much to me.'

'No. I don't think they know. He told me himself once. A long time ago and when he was in a funny old mood. After a bit to drink, perhaps. It was when I was supposed to come here with the grain but there was some reason why I couldn't. I told him and he said I had to. Said he damn well wasn't going himself.'

Grainger spoke slowly and there were long pauses during which they walked along without saying anything. They reached a five-bar gate which opened on to an avenue of trees. At the top of the avenue was a cluster of flint outbuildings. Beyond them the house itself. Tall and empty-looking.

'Is the lady there now?' asked Imogen.

'No. She sold up and left. I don't know who's in there now. But when she was there Balik knew her well. They had an understanding. You know what I mean? To be married.'

'Married?' Imogen couldn't imagine Mr Balik married to anyone. Or even with an 'understanding' to be married.

'It never came to it, though,' said Grainger, leaning on the gate. 'He lost her. That's the way he put it. She was lost.'

Suddenly the image of her mother's photograph in its wooden frame came to her. And Dad standing at the kitchen door with his back to her, looking out at the kiln-room.

'Did she die?' she asked.

'No. Not that sort of lost. She just went away.'

'To marry someone else?'

'I don't think so. But she was very young; just a girl. I suppose she might be married now.'

She tried to picture the girl with Mr Balik; tried to imagine them walking through lanes together. Nothing was very clear, though. She could see him, striding seriously along, frowning at the ground, but the girl wouldn't form properly in her mind. Did she walk in silence beside him? Or skip round him, showing him flowers and asking him all sorts of silly questions? Imogen almost saw a long, pale dress swinging along. She couldn't see a face. And anyway, perhaps, the picture she had of Mr Balik wasn't right either. Perhaps he wasn't so gloomy when he was with the girl.

'What has this got to do with me?' she said.

'You see them low buildings up there? A sort of barn and stables? She kept birds in one of them.'

Imogen narrowed her eyes and looked up the avenue. She could make out three rectangles constructed out of flint boulders, with perhaps a fourth tucked away in the background. They were old and heavy, each one topped with a sagging roof of dark slates. No. One roof was a little different from the others. Its slates looked clean and straight, as if it had been rebuilt.

'It was kind of a thing with her,' said Grainger. 'The birds. Hawks, like people used to hunt with. And an owl. He never told me this himself but some of the men at the grain store knew about it. They told me. All Balik ever said was that an owl always put him in mind of this lady. But he said that in drink, too. I'm sure he don't remember speaking of it.'

'A tame owl?'

'No. Of course not. You don't tame birds like that. But it was hers and it must've meant a lot to her. So, when I see the owls you brought up with your old man, well, it put me in mind of this lady. Balik asked you for them, then, did he?'

'Yes. When he came into the shop for the rent.'

'I wondered if he said anything. Told you anything.'

'No. Nothing.'

'It was just a bit of chance, then?'

'Yes.'

He was chewing his lip and staring at the distant house with nothing more to add, it seemed.

'Who was the lady?' Imogen asked eventually.

'Who was she?'

'Her name, I mean.'

'I don't know. It was just before my time with him and he only talked about her the once. He's not the sort of man you ask questions.'

'Why didn't they marry?'

'Don't know that, either,' he said, suddenly looking straight at her. 'Something went wrong. She went her way and he went his. She was a bit of a hot-headed sort by all accounts. But Balik took it hard. Had more to drink than he should. Raged about on his own.'

'But all this was before you knew him?'

'Whatever happened up here was before I knew him. But he was still likely to fly into rages when I come to manage the farmland for him. I thought the birds come into it somewhere but that's only my guess. And you don't know anything about it, either?'

'No.'

'No. I just wondered. He was sort of forgetting about it, as far as I could tell. Sort of settling down, I suppose. Till you turned up with them owls.' He breathed in deeply and looked back at the house. 'Now it looks like it's starting up again,' he said.

When Imogen got back to the house, Aunt Helen was nowhere to be seen. She went through to the kitchen where a series of echoing smacks filtered in from the garden. Her aunt was in the middle of wrestling with the rugs, flinging them over the line and beating clouds of dust out of them. Imogen tapped on the window and waved. She went outside to help.

'Look at all this,' said Aunt Helen. 'Just look at it all! This is what Jack's walked in from work. There's enough flour in these rugs to make a dozen rolls.'

She sighed and propped the beater against a hedge.

'And what did you find in Melling?' she asked with a sidelong glance at her niece. 'Plenty of mystery and excitement?'

'It's an interesting place if you're not used to it.'

'Oh, is it? You'll have to tell me all about that, my girl. I could just do with a bit of interest.'

'You go in and put the kettle on,' said Imogen with a smile. 'I'll take over for a bit.'

She set about the rugs, glad to make such a noise with the beater that Aunt Helen couldn't ask her any more questions.

9

'And how was old Jack?' Dad asked. 'Still the same?'

'He looked the same but he never said much. I couldn't tell.'

'No. He's a dark old horse, is Jack.'

He chuckled and nodded towards the teapot, meaning did she want another mug? Imogen shook her head. She'd said nothing about meeting Grainger. It was probably all in her aunt's note so it would come up in good time. As much of it as she wanted to tell.

'Aunt Helen loaded you up with supplies, as usual,' he said. 'Fruit loaves and jam and whatever.'

'She likes to do all that. You know she does.'

'I know.'

There was a pause while he pulled a piece of bread from the loaf and squeezed it into a pellet. His features seemed to sag a little. The cheerfulness seeped out of him. He stood up with a sigh. Giving up, Imogen thought. If you can't get what you want by being jolly, you don't know what else to do, do you?

'I hope you were good to her, sweet. She's very fond of you, you know.'

'Did you think I'd be rude, then?' she asked him sharply.

'No. No, of course not.'

'I wasn't. I was truly grateful.'

'You look much better now. I told you a good rest . . .'

'Yes. I know.'

'Helen thinks I don't look after you,' he said.

'She's right,' said Imogen and, when he looked at her, added with a smile, 'I look after you.'

Fortune was still on the window ledge in her room. Facing out, staring at the tree tops, as he had been over a week before. Imogen stood in the doorway for a moment, looking at him.

'Hallo,' she said, and then crossed the room to touch him lightly on his folded wings.

He was hard and cold; more so than she remembered. She let her fingers remain there and closed her eyes. Nothing happened, but she wasn't sure that she expected anything to.

'I'm coming to bed,' she told him. 'It tires you out, sitting on a cart for hours with old Basil Robinson, looking at fields. If anything happens,' she added slowly, 'I won't be afraid. I won't mean to be afraid, anyway. If I see anything. Or hear anything. I'll just keep still and listen. And see what happens.'

The night passed peacefully, though. Imogen was aware of Fortune, standing there in the shadows, silent and watchful. But he had nothing to say to her. No dreams came. Nothing at all.

In the morning his silhouette against the window square was the first thing she saw. Her lips were sticky and closed after sleep. She opened them to speak to him but changed her mind. Suddenly, she felt it would be a silly thing to do. Making him seem like some old toy, like the rag-doll she'd stopped talking to last year.

Life returned to normal. Helping Dad with the usual duties in the kiln-room and the shop. Walking past the empty school and thinking, dully, that she would be back there soon, to complete her last few weeks as a pupil. She remembered sitting on the beach and watching the expanse of the sea that made everything in the village seem so small and ordinary. But watching the sea was stuck in the past. Not last week but some distant, unreal time. She felt it had nothing to do with her now. And that incident with Grainger – the fear of him following her, the moment when she'd pushed him, his strange story about Mr Balik – all that seemed unreal too.

She walked past Old Carter's cottage one afternoon and Boy was sitting on the step with his arms round the dog's neck. Out of habit she veered away from him but he looked up and called to her.

'Hallo, Imogen. Where've you been, then?'

'Away. Nowhere special.'

'The seaside?'

'Maybe.'

He jumped up and fell in beside her. The dog crouched and sprang, yapping at his heels.

'Can't you keep him quiet?' she said.

'He's all right. He don't mean nothing. You're just saying hallo, aren't you, boy?'

'Hallo, dog,' Imogen said coldly. She narrowed

her eyes at the dog, wondering whether, perhaps, they shared some secret.

'I went there once,' Boy was saying. 'To the seaside. There was nothing to do.'

'That's nothing different. You don't do anything here.'

'I do. I helped with the harvest.'

'I expect that's why it took so long this year,' she said.

'It didn't take long, Imogen. It was the normal time.'

Too dim to see the joke, she thought. She gave him a withering smile and headed for the shop.

'Is your old man down for the cricket?' Boy called after her.

'What?'

'The cricket up on old Balik's lawns.'

'I don't know anything about any cricket.'

'There's tons you don't know, then, isn't there? The vicar's bringing a side from the cathedral. Ted says God's playing for them so it's not fair.'

'Don't be so stupid.'

'Going in first. W. G. God. With a big long beard.'

Imogen laughed, in spite of herself. 'If you didn't have such a solid wooden head, you'd be wicked, you would,' she said.

'That's not wicked, Ginny. That could be true. God can do anything so He could play cricket for the vicar if He wanted to. Then your old man would have to bowl to him.'

'If he's playing.'

'He is. Grainger asked him to last week.'

'Then why did you ask, if you know so much?'

'Just to see,' said Boy turning and wandering off.

Imogen let herself into the shop where Dad was wiping plates with a cloth and stacking them on a shelf.

'What's he been on about?' he asked. 'Has he been saying things to you?'

'Just going on in the usual way,' she said, passing straight through the shop.

'I could have a word with his mother. She'd sort him out.'

'No, Dad. It's not like that,' she called from the kitchen. 'He's only talking. He says you're going to play cricket against God and the vicar.'

'He said what?'

Dad set down his plates and put his head round the kitchen door, but Imogen was already out in the yard, and still smiling to herself. It was the first time anyone from school had called her Ginny.

After supper, Dad sat himself at the kitchen table and began to dab white liquid on a pair of old cricket boots. Imogen left the plates to drain at the sink and came to watch. She'd never seen the boots before. They were made of canvas, stiff and streaked greenish and pale brown at the toes. The hard leather of their soles shone and was curved like the bottoms of boats.

'I didn't know you ever played cricket,' she said, leaning over him to light the oil lamp.

'I used to. When you were a kiddie. Don't you remember?'

'Not a thing. Are you any good?'

'Grainger says I'm the only man that can turn a

ball properly,' he told her. 'Must be the clay. Working with my fingers all day.'

She sat opposite him and watched him work. The thought of the cricket match pleased him; he was almost talkative.

'It doesn't make any sense,' Imogen said. 'How can you turn a ball?'

'You impart spin on it.' He picked up a cup to demonstrate. 'Flick it in your fingers, like this, and it'll deviate off the pitch.'

'Like that? It'd fly off all over the place.'

'Not if you know what you're about it wouldn't.'

'Will you beat them, then?'

'We shall see. It won't be easy. The vicar played at Cambridge as a youth and clergymen can be devils with bat and ball, Imogen. Anyway, it's not the winning that counts. It's a social occasion. People get together and talk.'

'About cricket?' she laughed. 'That shouldn't delay them much.'

'About all kinds of things. It can be a very relaxed affair, can a match like this.'

'Can it? On Mr Balik's land?'

'I don't see why not.'

Of course, Imogen knew she'd have to go to the match. For Dad's sake. The thought of Mr Balik seeing her, though, on his lawns and so close to the house, was an uncomfortable one. The next morning she decided to take a walk up the hill to look at the house from the roadway. Just to look, to see how she felt about it. She had no intention of setting foot on Mr Balik's land a moment before she had to.

It was a quiet morning. There was no one about. She stood by the gate and looked up the drive. Then she remembered, you could see nothing of the house from here. Not when the trees were in full leaf. Just the drive leading into a green tunnel. She stayed there for a moment, looking and thinking. There were no odd feelings, no foreboding.

If I was a dog, she thought, it might be different.

She was about to return to the village when she caught sight of a figure standing under the trees in the drive. Not moving, but looking at her. After a moment of uncertainty, she saw that it was Grainger. She was sure that he recognized her but he gave no sign, not even a nod. He simply lowered his head and began to walk briskly away, down the curve of the drive towards the house. He was almost out of sight when he stopped, turned round and came back, just as briskly, in Imogen's direction. It reminded her of standing outside The Anchor with him; how he crossed the road before he could bring himself to say anything.

As if he can't speak at all when people are near, she thought.

And now he came to a halt, still a couple of yards off, still safe on Mr Balik's land, with the open gate a barrier between them. Even so, he was close enough for Imogen to make out the wiry grey hairs on his cheeks and lines like cracks running down from the corner of his mouth.

'Hallo, Imogen,' he said awkwardly.

She smiled at him. 'Are you all right now, Mr Grainger?' she asked.

He shuffled round, ignoring the question or perhaps not even hearing it properly, and looked off into the trees somewhere.

'You got some spare time?' he asked. 'To look at something in the house?'

'In the house?'

'Not indoors. Something you can see from the windows.'

'I don't know.'

'Balik won't know. He's out,' he said, and looked directly at her.

So Imogen stepped warily off the public highway and joined him in Mr Balik's drive. She followed a pace or two behind Grainger, her eyes fixed on the house as it came steadily into view. First a flat, grey corner of façade against the sky. Then a black square of window. The top of a column. Carving; leaves or something. She thought that was odd, somehow out of place. Carved to please someone's eye, yet almost out of sight.

'There,' said Grainger, stopping so abruptly that she almost ran into him. 'See?'

'What?'

'That window.'

He was pointing at a ground floor window. At first Imogen could make out nothing but the sheen of glass across several small squares. She moved a little to one side. The window became dark and she knew for certain that it was the dining room. She recognized the owl she'd seen on that night. It had been moved, placed against the glass, not quite in the middle of the ledge. It looked small and dainty against such a slab of black.

'You see it?' said Grainger.

'Yes, but . . .'

'It's facing out. Looking at us. Is that right?'
'I don't know.'
'I mean, is that how it's supposed to be?' His voice was urgent and he didn't wait for an answer. 'And look there, too. And there. And there.'
He jerked his arm from window to window. At each one stood one of the owls, facing outwards, its back to the dark of Mr Balik's house.
'You don't see it, Imogen? He always had them on them window ledges. Tidily placed, all looking square into the rooms. Now they've been moved. Turned round to face the grounds.'
'That's not strange, though,' said Imogen. 'It's what I've done.'
'What?' He looked sharply at her. 'You done it?'
'No, I mean . . . I don't think there's anything wrong with it. If I had owls I might have them like that. So they can see the trees and things.'
Grainger shook his head and she thought he was going to laugh at her for being so fanciful.
'Not shoved there any old how, you wouldn't, girl,' he said. 'See how he's done it. Just turned them round and stuck them against the glass. And look here.'
He strode away from her, towards the house, and leaned up to place the flat of his hand on one of the dining room windows. Imogen moved closer to look. She felt safer by Grainger's side.
'See this one?' he said. 'He's banged it down so hard it's cracked the pane. I'll have to see to that but I can't say anything to Balik, can I? It's like telling him, look what you've done. Like asking him what he's up to.'
'I don't know what to say, Mr Grainger.'

'You can't explain it to me?'

'No.'

He breathed in deeply through his nose before adding, 'Well, there's other things, too.'

'What other things?'

'Writing.'

'Writing?'

'He sits up half the night writing stuff on paper. And then screwing it up and burning most of it. Why should he take to doing that?'

'I don't know.'

'And shouting. The night before last. I come out of my room at the back to fetch something from the kitchen, and there's shouting going on in the dining room.'

'Mr Balik shouting?'

'There's no one else here.'

'But it was him?'

'Of course it was him. Yelling out something or other, like he was scared. I couldn't make it out. And there was no one else about, that I'm sure of.'

'What happened?'

'Nothing, as far as I could tell. I didn't hang around to ask. Then, in the morning, I goes through the house and sees these things, all moved.' He paused and looked at her. 'Thought you might know something about it.'

'I'm sorry Mr Grainger,' she said firmly. 'I don't understand either.'

'No,' he said and looked at her in silence for a moment. 'I didn't know who else to talk to, though. Things go from bad to worse with him, you see, and I don't know how they'll end up.'

'I'm sorry,' Imogen said again.

There was nothing more she could say to Grainger. She could see that it perplexed him and she wanted both to help and to understand for her own sake.

'One more thing,' he said, shrugging as if, now that he'd asked her, it didn't matter any more. 'In the workshop.'

He set off round the side of the house and Imogen followed reluctantly. As soon as she lost sight of the drive she became anxious that Mr Balik might return. She could picture him riding up to the front door, swinging from the saddle and shouting for Grainger. Finding her there. The surprise and anger in his face.

The workshop was an old wooden shed which slouched against the back wall of the house. It looked as if it had been dumped there until a better place could be found for it. The planks of the old door were dark and rotten from contact with the damp ground. Grainger ducked his head and went in.

'Wait there,' he said. 'I won't be a moment.'

Imogen peered after him into the gloom. Grainger's private place. It suited him, she thought. A floor of trodden earth; a heavy bench, solid like the stump of a tree that had grown there; a scattering of tools; shelves of tins and jars. In one corner she noticed a pot of brown glue like the one Dad kept in the kiln-room. She waited, heard Grainger clear his throat, glanced back at the corner of the house, expecting Balik to appear at any moment. She wanted to run. Her nails were digging into her palms. She called Grainger's name but couldn't make it loud enough for him to hear.

Eventually he emerged with a small parcel of blue sugar paper which he held out to her. She didn't know whether she should take it.

'Apples,' he explained with a nod. 'Good 'uns. He won't miss 'em.'

'Thank you,' she said uncertainly.

'A couple for you. And one for the potter. If he likes. Tell him we're in for rain.'

'In for rain?'

'That's right. The pitch could turn a treat.'

He grinned at her, showing two brown teeth. Then went back into the shed.

On the Friday evening, the day before the match, Imogen went up to her room and saw at once that the window was ajar and that the ledge was empty. She thought that perhaps she had opened the window herself but she knew that she hadn't touched the owl. She looked quickly, helplessly round the room. It had not been disturbed. She went down to the kitchen again.

'What's the matter?' asked Dad, looking up from a book and seeing something wrong in Imogen's face.

'Did you go into my room today?'

'Why should I do that?'

'Did you?'

'Of course not. I don't go to your room unless I tell you first. You know that. Not since . . .'

He didn't finish but she knew what he was trying to say. Not since that time he'd half-heartedly tried to pack for her trip to Melling.

'Is anything wrong, sweet?'

'I was looking for something,' she said.

'What?'

'It doesn't matter. It's not important. I just thought . . .'

'Do you want me to look for you?'

'No. It'll turn up.'

She went back to her room and stood at the window, looking out at the trees and the roof of the kiln-room, listening keenly. The night was still. There was a muddle of distant singing from The Hope but no other sound.

On that other occasion, when Fortune had flown out into the night, there had been the rattle of his wings, a disturbance which seemed deliberate, as if he'd wanted her to know what he was doing. This time there was only absence and silence. She reached for her mother's cloak on the back of the door, as she had done before. Then stopped, let her arm drop. What was the point of going outside now? The only place to look for him, she felt sure, would be Mr Balik's house and she couldn't go there until Dad was asleep. That might be another hour or so. And supposing she did go. What could she do up there? What could she achieve? She would be powerless. A witness, perhaps; nothing more.

She stretched out on her bed, fully clothed, and stared at the ceiling.

Maybe he's simply gone, she thought suddenly. Maybe Fortune didn't mean to come back.

10

Grainger's promise of rain came to nothing. The Saturday of the match was bright and clear. Imogen was putting together some food to take with them to Mr Balik's grounds.

'There's been a heavy dew, though,' Dad called down the stairs. 'Might prove beneficial, I suppose. Give a bit of grip to the soil. And the sun'll make a nice day of it, won't it?'

Imogen didn't answer. She packed the sandwiches into a basket and thought about the thirteenth owl. Missing him. Now that he'd gone, now that she knew he wasn't waiting on her window ledge, the day felt dull, as if a mist had closed on it. Dad's voice and the familiar sounds of the plates, the knives and forks against the kitchen table, all seemed muffled and more ordinary than they had been before. But relief was part of this, too. The sense that a vague worry had been removed. The world had become safe again; safe and predictable.

Dad clattered downstairs and appeared before her at the kitchen door. Dazzling, almost like an angel.

'Well,' he said. 'Do I look the part?'

He held out his arms awkwardly, allowing

Imogen to inspect him. She laughed in spite of herself.

'Very smart,' she said. 'You look too white to be running around and sweating. What's that round your waist?'

'That tie. You know, the one Helen gave me.'

'Oh Dad . . .'

'I know, I know, but I'm never going to wear it round my neck, Imogen. And I don't like to tell Helen I've never even had it on, and I don't like to lie . . .'

'So now you can say you've worn it, in all truth?'

'And that it looked the proper thing.'

He smiled widely and started to turn round on his heels, so she could see the back.

'Yes, very smart,' she said again. 'You could go off and get married in an outfit like that.'

Stupid, she thought to herself as soon as she'd said it. A stupid thing to say. She glanced at the fading photograph above the kitchen fireplace. A quick look, then away again. Dad stopped turning, just for a second, with his back still to her. He lowered his head and she saw his neck stretch. It was brown and pitted, like the cover of their bible. When he turned back to her again he was smiling. Not quite the same, but still smiling.

'We'd better go,' he said. 'I want a good look at the opposition before we start.'

'The very sight of you will strike fear into their hearts,' she told him, reaching up to straighten his collar.

A pitch had been prepared on the wide lawns to the back of the house and a large marquee erected in a space between two flowerbeds. Dad went off to talk to the rest of the team, leaving Imogen to find a place to sit. She walked slowly round the boundary, looking for somewhere out of the way, hoping that she would see no signs of Mr Balik. She was so intent on this that Boy had shouted to her twice before she noticed him.

'You come to learn a thing or two, then, Imogen?'

He was leaning against the trunk of a poplar, tugging at an impossibly long boot lace. She wandered over to him.

'Are you playing, too, Boy?'

'I am now. They were a man short.' He didn't look up. He was concentrating proudly on his lace. 'Old Grainger come down and asked me himself.'

'You? They're still a man short, then, aren't they?' she said with a wide-eyed look he couldn't see.

'No. That's what I'm saying. It's me. I've filled in.'

'Of course.' She smiled at him. 'Good luck, Boy,' she said and began to walk away again.

'Oi. Ginny. Look at this.'

When she turned round she saw him jumping about, crashing both feet down flat and hard, and grinning fiercely.

'A good bit of tresp-arse this is. Eh?'

'We're all invited,' she told him. 'It's not trespass if you're invited.'

'I don't care. I just like treading on his grass. I only wish he could see it.'

'He might see it, the way you're carrying on. Everyone else is looking at you.'

'He's not going to see, though,' Boy said, stopping. 'He's gone away for the day.'
'Where to?'
'Melling. So Mr Grainger said.'
'Melling? Are you sure?'
'I'm always sure. Anyway, why shouldn't he be there?'
'I just didn't think he ever . . .'
'What?'
'It doesn't matter. Good luck, Boy. I hope you do well.'
Imogen was glad that Mr Balik wouldn't be around; but knowing where he'd gone made her feel uneasy. Why Melling? Didn't Grainger say he never went to Melling, that he hadn't been there for years? So why had he gone there today? If he wanted to keep out of the way of the crowds at the cricket match he could've gone almost anywhere; out into the fields, even somewhere in the depths of the house. But not Melling.
She found somewhere to sit where she could keep her back to the high, grey walls and blank windows of the house. Even with the master out of the way, she didn't want to see it every time she lifted her head to watch the cricket.
Grainger went in first for the village, holding himself straight and still and gently patting his bat on the ground. Everyone was turned his way; the fielders, the watchers spread round the boundary with their boxes and rugs, even the ring of dark trees behind them. There he stood, the imposing centre of a green circle, not at all like the Grainger Imogen was used to seeing.
Everything became still as the game started. The

only movement was the soft tapping of the bat on the ground and the leaning run of the bowler hurrying in to the wicket. Imogen hardly saw the ball leave the bowler's hand. She heard him grunt as he swung his arm, saw Grainger lift on to his toes then turn and look over his shoulder. The ball appeared, bobbling down towards the boundary, and only then, it seemed, did Imogen hear the chock of its impact on the bat.

'Yes,' shouted the batsman at the other end. Grainger loped up the wicket and the match was under way.

As it unfolded, Imogen tried to take an interest in the cricket but she found it impossible to tell which side was winning. Instead she became distracted by the efforts of Mr Bailey who was supposed to be scoring. From time to time he would run backwards and forwards to the large black score-board, then stand still with his eyes shut and one hand clasped to the top of his head as he tried to remember the score.

'Score-board! Score-board!' figures in white yelled to him from the distance. 'Try to keep it up to date, will you?'

Whenever Imogen looked back to the cricket a clergyman with a boyish face and shiny black hair seemed to be bowling in a cartwheel of arms and legs. Occasionally he managed to get a ball through to rattle the stumps or to thump against someone's legs. Then he would lift both arms in the air and twist round to shout like a pagan at the umpire. At other times Grainger would move forward, make a seemingly gentle arc with his bat and the ball would go scudding over the grass to the boundary.

The day wore on like this, the odd flurry of excitement and long stretches of repeated rituals. Dad went in to bat, swung one ball away to the trees for four and sent another steepling into the sky. Their own vicar placed himself beneath it and waited with his hand cupped before his face. Imogen heard the slap of the ball against his palms, saw him buckle a little at the knees. And Dad was out. He trudged back to where the village team had scattered their gear, nodding briefly to the vicar as he passed but not looking in Imogen's direction at all.

Boy's turn came last. The black-haired clergyman slowed his run considerably but still managed to send a ball into the pit of Boy's stomach. Both teams gathered round him and several clergymen ruffled his hair. He then went back to the crease, closed his eyes and nicked the next delivery over the wicket-keeper's head. The ball skimmed over the grass towards Imogen. A rural dean, his face red and shiny, came galloping after it. He was running straight for her, baring his teeth as if he meant to savage her. When he saw his chase was useless, he struggled to a standstill. The ball trickled over the boundary and Imogen bent to scoop it up and toss it back to him.

It was at that moment, as the ball was about to roll into her hand, that she sensed someone move behind her. A shadow appeared on the grass to her left. More than a shadow, in fact; darker, as if it had a substance of its own. She stood slowly and turned round.

Mr Balik, in a long black coat and dark riding trousers, shielding his eyes against the sun.

The world seemed to slow down. She felt the leather of the ball in her fingers. Mr Balik, silhouetted in a gap of blue between the corner of the house and a line of trees, moved his head. Imogen couldn't see his eyes but she knew he was looking at her.

'Young lady. Young lady, can you hear me?'

The rural dean was calling to her. The top of his head was pink with sweat and he was holding out his hand for the ball.

'Oh, yes,' she said blankly. 'I'm sorry.'

He might've been standing there for minutes. She couldn't tell. She smiled at him, saw his eyes take in the scar on her cheek as he smiled back.

As the clergyman galloped back to the game, Imogen turned her head and saw Mr Balik out of the corner of her eye. He was still looking at her. Then there was something small and solid bisecting the patch of sky above his head.

A curving, steady flight, from the trees to the house. Like an omen, a shooting star. Not silver on black as a star should have been, but some dark thing against the bright day-blue.

Mr Balik twisted round and looked up, too. But he couldn't have seen anything. The sky was empty again.

Shortly after that Boy was bowled and the players all came in for lunch.

'Eighty-four to get,' said Grainger striding towards the marquee. 'They won't find it easy if we can keep it straight. They'll have to fight hard for it.'

Imogen followed him and stood at the entrance, looking through the pale gloom for Dad. She saw him perch astride a bench and tap a place for Boy to sit next to him. The sun on the canvas made their faces appear blue, almost as if they were under water.

'Put yourself down there, Boy,' said Dad. 'Eat with the men. That four of yours might yet decide the whole thing.'

Imogen was relieved to see him laugh. He didn't look as if he needed the company of his daughter. Mrs Carter hurried past her with a plate of sandwiches.

'That master of yours turned up after all,' she said to Grainger. 'I thought you told us he'd be at Melling all day.'

'I did, because he was. So he said to me, anyway.'

'Well, he's back.'

'Then I'd better see what he wants.'

Grainger's face assumed his usual frown. If he felt that there was anything to worry him about Mr Balik's early return, he kept it to himself. He clambered awkwardly out of his place and headed in the direction of the house. Again Imogen followed him, this time keeping her distance so that he wouldn't notice her. She saw him take the path through the circular herb garden and step down on to the lower lawn. Then stop and look up.

Mr Balik was standing at an upper window. His face stood out against the darkness of his coat and the room behind him. Grainger was familiar with that look, knew better than to interrupt. He turned and went back to the marquee. Imogen shrank back and let him pass.

Between his fingers Mr Balik was holding a sheet of paper. After a second he closed his fist on it, screwed it into a ball and tossed it aside. Then stood there, looking out at distance. Not taking anything in. Below him on the ground floor, she could see one of his owls at the dining room window.

It stood on the ledge as if it, too, were staring out at nothing.

During the afternoon, the vicar's team were all out for eighty, four runs short, and Dad took four of the wickets. Four wickets, including that of the vicar himself. He described each one to Imogen, endlessly, as they collected up their things and left the ground.

'I paid the vicar back for catching me out,' he said, his eyes sparkling. 'The ball shot off like I was bowling on a pebble beach, Imogen. Do you understand what I mean? The way the ball deviated from its line?'

'Yes, Dad.'

'I shall feel the stiffness tomorrow, you can bet on that. Worth it, though. Worth every ache and pain.'

She was hardly listening but he was too pleased with his afternoon's work to notice. They entered the tunnel of trees over Mr Balik's drive. Several paces ahead of them Old Carter walked with Boy who was trailing his sweater along the ground behind him. Beyond them, just passing through the gate and turning into the lane, were the vicar and Mrs Carter. As Dad rambled on, Imogen looked up to see a dark movement, a flutter against the pale canopy of leaves. The same dark movement she'd seen earlier, above Mr Balik's head, only clearer now, bigger.

Something had settled on the iron gate.

No one else saw it. Old Carter had stopped to remonstrate with Boy. Dad was staring down at the ground while he talked.

Imogen couldn't stop herself calling out.

'Look,' she said. 'On the gate.'

'What? What is it?'

But almost at once the bird lifted off again. That familiar leap, the hunch and then the take-off. It swooped up the drive towards them, over their heads and out of sight towards the house.

'Did you see it?'

'Only just,' said Dad. 'A crow or something.'

'No. Not a crow. It was an owl.'

'Couldn't have been, sweet. It's too early for most owls.'

'But it was. I saw it.'

'The only sort you'd see in daytime,' Dad said resolutely, 'would be little owls and that would be too big for a little owl.'

He hadn't seen it properly but that didn't matter. He didn't want to believe that it was an owl. Imogen said no more about it. She wondered whether he was right. A crow, and not an owl. Perhaps she'd seen a crow and her imagination had told her it was an owl.

Old Carter was waiting for them to catch up.

'Nice bit of bowling, potter,' he said. 'They couldn't tell ball from grass when you were on.'

'Thank you, Carter. I did my best.'

'Well, it was good enough. A famous victory, I'd've said. It should help to keep the Church's feet on the ground.'

The two men walked side by side and Dad began

to tell Carter all about the capturing of his wickets. Boy fell in beside Imogen.

'I took one in the belly. Did you see?'

She didn't answer.

'Nearly got me in the pills, too. Didn't think vicars were supposed to do things like that. What's the matter?'

'Boy, did you see that bird on the gate?'

'Just now? Yes. Why?'

'It really was there?'

''Course it was. Then it flew up to Balik's place. You can go anywhere when you're a bird. That'd be good, that would. If I was a bird I wouldn't go anywhere near . . .'

'What was it?'

'What?'

'What sort of bird was it?'

'I don't know . . .'

'It was an owl, Boy. You saw it. You were closer than we were. You must've . . .'

'It couldn't have been an owl, Imogen. It didn't have proper feathers. And it was all kind of shiny.'

11

She went up to her room, closed the door carefully, and it began to happen just as she feared it would. The dream came back more fiercely than ever before.

She stretched out on the bed but knew she wouldn't sleep. She only had to close her eyes for the images to swoop around her head.

The man-bird in black, with its gaping, silent beak.

The flames in corridors.

And Fortune muddled in with it all.

He was leaning forward and swinging his head from side to side. Mr Balik was there, too. Looking out at her from the upstairs window. At times his face took the place of the man-bird's face. Instead of the beak there was Mr Balik's mouth, wide open and shouting but making no sound. A point of gold at his collar, shining in the dark. The skin tight over bulging eyes in a face that was both Mr Balik's and the man-bird's.

And then the eyes began to split, like the skin of a chestnut. Suddenly there was blackness staring out at her and all around her a low, throbbing sound. It was a humming, singing noise but there was no word behind it, nothing that made any human sense.

Nevertheless, Imogen understood what it meant. That it was calling her.

It was only when she stopped at the end of Mr Balik's drive that she realized that the sound had disappeared and the night was quiet. Cloud cleared from the face of the moon for a moment and made the grass between her and the house a silver-grey. She looked back over her shoulder and wondered whether she should go home again. It felt wrong to be here. Why had she come? Nothing made any sense.

Then she noticed that one of the dining-room windows was open and she knew that Fortune was inside somewhere. That, at least, made sense.

She moved out of the shadow of the trees and made quickly for the house. Her cloak flapped heavily behind her and she felt a few warm drops of the promised rain on her hands and face. By the time she reached the window it was raining steadily. There was darkness and emptiness inside the house.

She waited for a while, thinking hard but deciding nothing.

Then she reached up, hooked her fingers over the ledge and pulled herself in. Her boots scrabbled at the wall and then she was tumbling into the room. One elbow struck the floor with a thud. She lay there for a second or two, listening, and looked around the room.

It was large. High and narrow, with only one or two pieces of furniture: a solid, carved sideboard near to where she'd fallen; a long dining table and some tall-backed chairs, all black as iron. She stood up carefully and began to walk round the table. There were several sheets of paper scattered across it. Some screwed into balls. Matches and a stub of candle. A pen and an ink stand.

No sign of what she was looking for.

'Fortune?' she said. No more than a breath.

The only other sound in the room was the beating of rain on the windows. She couldn't see him.

At the far end of the table were two plates, abandoned half way through a meal. Soft white in the gloom. She was looking at them when her foot pressed on something and she couldn't prevent herself putting her full weight on it. It slipped and crunched, like a man's hand. She froze and looked down.

Bones.

'Dear God,' she said quickly to herself.

But they were chicken bones, tossed on to the floor and left there, and she shut her eyes and sighed.

Then a shriek. A blade of sound cutting the night. Filling the room, shriek and echo almost in the same moment.

Where? Where from?

Imogen cried out and twisted round. She saw a rounded, gravestone shape by a circular mirror on the sideboard. Something like a lowered head, looking at her. She saw the dark of eyes, the arch of a back in the mirror. Had she found him? Was he looking directly at her now?

For some moments everything remained still. Then there was a violent disturbance of air, coming across the room towards her. It lifted a sheet of paper from the table and floated it to the floor.

Imogen cowered, throwing up her arms to protect her face. But nothing touched her. For an instant a kind of darkness hung above her head before rising and passing over to the window ledge behind her.

When she turned she saw Mr Balik's owl, and next to it a kind of pulsing shadow, seeming to step from side to side.

'Fortune,' she said softly.

Then the movement stopped. She peered through the gloom but all she could see was the ordinary pottery owl, motionless on the ledge. By itself.

'No. Don't leave me,' she called.

She ran to the open window, catching the chicken bone with her foot and spinning it across the floor to clatter against a chair leg. She leaned right out of the window and called again.

'Where are you?'

There was no answer. Warm rain hit her face in thick drops and the smell of soaked earth rose up to her. Nothing moved behind the curtain of falling water.

She turned back to the room, almost crying with frustration.

'Why have you brought me here?' she said, dropping to her knees. 'What is it you want?'

On the floor before her was the sheet of paper which had fallen from the table. She picked it up. Scratched across the top in black ink was a single word.

Charlotte.

Imogen felt for the matches and lit the stub of candle. She breathed deeply once or twice. The circle of pale light on the table calmed her.

I shouldn't be feeling like this, she thought. Not here. I don't belong. Mr Balik's house. His words on paper. I should go home and mind my own business.

But she knew she had to stay. And read what she had found, what she had been led to.

She sat down, slowly and deliberately, and spread the paper on the table in front of her.

Charlotte. And, beneath it, a line gouged with such force that it had torn through the paper, and a block of black ink words in an urgent, neat hand.

Charlotte.

I have spoken your name again. I have said it out loud. I did not want to – I was afraid of the sound of your name – but it has been forced from me.

Charlotte.

After all these years I have been back to Melling. I rode there myself this morning, feeling sick at heart the nearer I got. I knew you would not be there. I do not know where you are but I knew I would not find you in Melling.

Every day since I destroyed your life I have thought about you. Many times I have asked the Lord to forgive me for what I did. He has not forgiven me. I have tried to forget but that does not work. Now I am making myself remember.

I wish you had cursed me for my sin. Your curse would have been easier to bear than your silence. But it is your silence that I deserve. It is what I have been living with all this time, the memory of that day and your silence.

Charlotte.

At times I have thought of looking for you, to confess and tell you of the remorse I feel. There is no courage in me, though. I was afraid of the look I might see in your face and I could not do it.

Lately I have been haunted by another fear; the fear that you are no longer alive. I cannot explain why I feel this. I do not understand it myself. That is why I am writing to you now. A letter I have started over and over again but will never send.

I see images of fire in the night, terrible images of fire and birds. I have imagined a bird at the window behind me. It seemed so real, flapping at the window as if it was trying to beat its way inside. It has caused me such torment that I could not think properly, did not know what to do with myself.

This is why I rode over to Melling. To make myself suffer. To punish myself with the sight of the place where we had been happy. And your name.

Charlotte.

Today I stood at the end of the drive and looked at your house again. I remembered the things I had said to you; how I had wanted you to be perfect, to belong to me, to be tamed. And I remembered that night; when I shouted at you for not being what I wanted, and ran out of the house with my head full of my own anger.

I made myself remember everything I did.

How I ran blindly into the stable. How I snatched a saddle from its peg and threw it down in my rage.

I saw it all again.

The oil lamp falling against the bale of straw. The sudden sheet of flame. And me standing there, a hopeless coward, not knowing what to do.

Oh, Charlotte.

I saw your birds tethered to their perches and beating their wings in panic.

I should have stayed in that fire and tried to save them. It would have been better to stay and be eaten up by the flames.

I remember the terrible silence the last time I saw you. How you would not look at me.

Charlotte.

Oh, Charlotte . . .

12

Imogen sat for some while staring at the paper, unable to move or think at all clearly. She was feeling small and full of shame at what she had done. Then she heard a sound outside the room. A board cracking under a footfall, very sharp. She brought her hand down abruptly on the pale flame. The room became darker than ever and hot wax burnt into her palm. She dropped to her knees and crawled under the table, pulling up the hood of the cloak to hide her yellow hair.

The door opened and a shimmer of light came into the room. A candle trembled in the draught from the window. Two or three heavy steps across the floor. Her arms and legs began to shake and she squeezed her hands between her knees.

'What is it?' That familiar, dark voice, very low. 'What do you want?'

Imogen held her breath as Mr Balik strode round the table to the open window. He paused and turned slowly so that Imogen could hear his boots scrape minutely on the boards.

'You?' he said softly.

She stood up, as steadily as she could. Her heart was pounding but there was nothing else she could do. She'd have to face him now. Then she saw that his back was to her. Still staring out of the window. No. Not out but at the window. At the pottery owl, motionless on the ledge. He didn't know she was in the room with him.

She turned to look for the door. Moved slowly towards it, slowly. And hit the back of a chair with her arm. The chair dragged across the floor, loud and sudden. Mr Balik jerked round, saw her and held the candle up. A lemon glow across the dome of his forehead. For a second they faced each other.

'Oh God,' he whispered. 'It can't be.'

He was staring at her as if she were somehow unreal. She wanted to look away but couldn't.

'What do you want from me?'

The silence was unbearable but there was nothing Imogen could say to him. It was as if two shadows faced each other.

'Speak to me,' he said, his voice low and trembling, his face full of pain and helplessness. 'If you can't forgive me, say something.'

The rain outside and nothing but rain.

'God save me, you're . . . you aren't alive any more. Is that why you've come? Because you're . . ? Have you come to punish me?'

The candle fell from his hand and spluttered out on the table. He stumbled away from her, backwards, awkwardly swinging his arm. It struck something behind him. The owl on the ledge. It teetered, rocked against the window, scratching the glass as it slid down and toppled to the floor.

And smashed. A high, sharp crack on the floor. The scattering of fragments.

Following by a roaring sound. Part shout, part

scream, as if something in Mr Balik had cracked, too.

He ran to the door, barging it open with his shoulder. Imogen heard his footsteps on floorboards, then on marble, then running up the stairs. The shouting faded into the depths of the house.

She hadn't moved since Mr Balik had turned to look at her. Now she was alone she groped for one of the dining chairs and sat down. She felt that she should do something. But what? A second crash sounded from somewhere above her head. Another owl, she guessed, smashed from its ledge. Then another. He was raging through the house, breaking them all.

A long sigh shook her body, as if she'd been holding her breath all this time, and she began to sob. She had no control over what was happening in this house and yet she felt that she was responsible for it. She didn't belong, and she knew things she had no right to know. The madness that had taken hold of Mr Balik was because of her. She'd followed Fortune up to the house and she'd brought destruction with her. The owls destroyed, Mr Balik destroyed, and in time she would be destroyed, too.

Another explosion sounded upstairs, a high-pitched cracking sound followed almost at once by the booming of a vast drum as something hit the floorboards. For a while she heard nothing but then there came the sounds of quick, sudden movements in one of the upstairs rooms. Followed by silence again.

She felt her way carefully to the door of the dining room and looked out. She recognized the hall where they'd first brought the owls, all those weeks ago.

She could just make out the pattern of squares on the floor. The old planks still propped by the wall. Rain was washing down the tall windows, smearing everything inside with a weak, grey light. A broad marble staircase led up to deep shadows. And out of these shadows came a white face, as if it had no body. It began to move smoothly down the stairs. Became clearer, Mr Balik carrying something like a rod against his shoulder. At first Imogen thought it was his silver-topped stick but it was more solid than that, with the dull sheen of metal.

She shrank back as he crossed the hall and threw open the double doors. A gust of lurid wind and rain blew in. He stepped outside and the doors banged to behind him.

Then Imogen was alone in the house. There was a release of silence all around her and the whole place suddenly seemed empty.

She backed into the dining room and felt her way to a window at the far end. From there, she thought, she would be able to see where Mr Balik was going. All she could make out, though, was a blur of movement behind diagonal canes of rain. Stooped and moving fast somewhere to the right. Towards the marquee, perhaps. She pressed her face against the glass but nothing was clear. All moving things seemed to be branches and shadows tossing in the wind.

Let him go, she thought. He's made this trouble for himself. Stay where you are and let him go.

She turned back to the table and stood for a while, touching the rim of one of the plates with her fingers. Looking down at it and thinking.

He has destroyed the owls and he will destroy you. Leave him alone.

On the other side of the room the shards of broken owl were scattered across the floor. She sensed them there in the darkness. Ruined.

She remained at the edge of the table for several moments, poised between two states of mind, the need to stay where she was and the need to act. She pictured Mr Balik stumbling blindly through the rain. Pictured the silent pieces of shattered pottery. The images came and went in her head.

A man in driving rain, a broken owl. Over and over.

Then, almost without thinking, she found herself hurrying towards the dining room door, blundering against a chair, running desperately across the hall.

Outside, the rain was toppling out of a black sky. It soaked through her cloak in seconds and made her slip as she ran. She reached the lawn by the marquee and stopped. There was thick mud down one thigh and the length of her arm, though she couldn't remember falling.

She saw Mr Balik's bowed back a few paces ahead of her. He was kneeling in the middle of the lawn, like a man at prayer, a penitent. She called his name but her voice was snatched away by the wind. She was about to shout again but something made her hesitate.

Surely it would be wrong to go stumbling up to him now. To break into his thoughts and tell him . . . What? She didn't know how to tell him who she was, why she was there.

Maybe it's best he thinks I'm someone else, she told herself. Best for him and best for me.

But as she watched she saw his back straighten. He seemed to feel her presence and he twisted slowly round to look at her through wide eyes.

His bunched fists gripping a shot-gun.

Its muzzle forced under his chin.

Not a man at prayer at all.

'Let me go.' His voice was low and rasping. 'I'll pay for what I've done. Let that be enough.'

'Mr Balik, no . . .'

Imogen took a step forward and sank to her knees, close enough to touch him now. He stiffened and tightened his grip on the gun.

'Keep away from me!'

'Can't you see?' she said, pulling back her hood. 'I'm not Charlotte. You've got things wrong . . .'

He stared back at her with water washing over his face. The rain bore down on them out of the darkness with a steady, beating sound.

'Mr Balik, it's me. Imogen. From the potter's shop.'

'Imogen . . .'

'You know me. We brought you the owls, Dad and me.'

One hand unfolded from the gun and he lifted it carefully to Imogen's face. She let him touch her lightly on the chin. And trace the scar on her cheek with his cold fingers. He studied her face like a man in a trance.

'What's happened to you?' he whispered. 'Your face . . .'

'I had an accident. When I was little.'

'No . . .'

'Yes, Mr Balik. My name is Imogen. I was burnt.'

'Burnt? In the fire?'

'No, no. On the kiln door. Here in the village. You know who I am.'

'The potter's girl,' he said to himself, and then frowned uncertainly. 'What are you doing here?'

'I don't know. There was . . . something calling me here.'

'Calling you? Who was it?'

'It wasn't a person, Mr Balik. I . . . I can't explain . . .'

'You must. Tell me what it was.'

'It was like an owl.'

'An owl,' he said slowly. 'Yes.'

His voice was weak and distracted. He lowered his head and looked at the gun resting against his chest. Imogen saw his white fingers trembling against the barrel.

'I've seen it, too,' he said.

'Please, Mr Balik . . .'

She lifted her hand gently towards him. Held it still. He watched her place it over his fingers.

Then, somewhere behind them, she heard the splash of heavy footsteps. Out of the corner of her eye she saw the huddled shape of Grainger hurrying towards them over the wet lawn.

'Wait,' she called without turning round.

Two, three heavy seconds hung between them before Mr Balik released his grip on the gun. He looked with astonishment in his eyes from Imogen to Grainger.

'Will you help me?' he mumbled. 'I don't know what I'm doing here.'

All Mr Balik's strength seemed to have left him. He hardly knew where he was and Grainger had to carry him in his arms like a child. He took him into the house and up to his room.

'You go ahead,' he told Imogen. 'Open the doors for me.'

Mr Balik's room was large and cool with a high ceiling. Imogen waited at the door while Grainger lifted his master on to the bed.

It took great strength, she thought, to move him as gently as that.

Out of the corner of her eye she saw something curved and jagged, like a piece of jawbone, in one of the corners. She guessed it was part of another broken owl.

Grainger took the corner of the coverlet and wiped mud and rain from Mr Balik's face.

'We'll leave him to himself for a bit,' he said, steering Imogen out into the corridor.

He closed the door softly behind him. Then sighed and narrowed his eyes at her.

'I can't tell you why I'm here, Mr Grainger,' she said firmly before he could speak. 'It's no good you asking.'

'Then you'd best go home, Imogen. And hope he forgets all about this.'

But she knew that Mr Balik would not forget, any more than she would. She also knew that she could not go home. There was one more thing that had to be done before she could leave the house that night.

13

Grainger stood an oil lamp on the dining room table. Next to it he placed the pot of brown glue Imogen had asked him to fetch from his workshop. Then he watched in silence as she gathered up the shards and fragments from the floor and arranged them in the pool of light.

'Is this what you must do?' he asked quietly.

'It is.'

'And it must be done now, must it? At this hour of the night?'

'I think it must, Mr Grainger, yes.'

'Then I'll say no more.'

It was slow and careful work and Imogen had no notion of how long it was taking her. Time seemed to have stopped moving. Her fingers wanted to hurry but she wouldn't let them. She had to do this properly.

Eventually the pieces were put together and there was a complete owl standing before her on the table. Then she took some of the glue and made a paste of dust and splinters which she smeared into the largest fissures running through its body. Grainger stood beyond the light and watched her in silence.

'So,' he said. 'It's finished.'

'Yes. One owl to begin with. It'll do for now.'

'It'll do well. Good as new.'

'Oh no, Mr Grainger. It's not that.'

Imogen knew that, if you looked closely at it, you could see a jigsaw of cracks and crazes across its body. It would never be as good as new again. She rubbed her eyes with the back of her hand. The rain had stopped and there was a yellow grey light at the windows.

Weak sunlight fell on the stairs and across the landing. She stood for several moments at the door to Mr Balik's room, watching him. His face was even paler than usual and there were thin strands of black hair stuck to his forehead. She couldn't tell whether he was awake or not until he spoke.

'I don't know what you're doing here,' he said, 'but I'm glad you came. I mean, I'm glad that it was you and not . . .'

'I know, Mr Balik.' She paused and took a breath. 'I . . . I think I know more than I ought to.'

'Do you?'

'About Charlotte, I mean . . .'

'Oh. The letter.'

'Yes. I'm sorry. I . . .'

'It doesn't matter.'

'I shan't say anything, Mr Balik.'

'No.' He smiled a faint, inward smile, not intended for her, and opened his eyes. 'I can't see you if you stand there with the light behind you.'

She stepped into the room and pushed the door to behind her.

'Look,' she said, holding up the owl for him to see. 'I've brought this for you.'

'What is it?'

She moved a little nearer. He blinked, to clear his eyes, and half lifted a hand, as if he wanted to touch it but didn't have the courage.

'Mended?' he said.

'Yes.'

'You did this?'

'Yes. You left it smashed, and now it's fixed.'

'Why did you do it?'

'It was something that had to be done. Can you see? Broken and mended. And better for it.'

'Better for it? How can it be?'

'It's not perfect any more. I know that. But that's not what I mean. It's different now, not like it was before. You can see the story of what's happened to it.'

Mr Balik remained still for such a long time that Imogen began to wonder whether he'd forgotten she was there.

'Put it down on that chest,' he said at last.

She placed it in a patch of light the shape of the window, and stood aside while he looked at it. Trying to see its story. How it had been in pieces, and was now a complete owl again. Imperfect but whole.

'The others can be mended, too,' she said. 'In time, if you agree to it.'

'Broken and mended,' he said to himself softly. 'Yes. The others, too.'

Grainger walked down the drive with Imogen and would have escorted her all the way home. She stopped by the iron gate, though, and said she'd prefer him to leave her there.

'Well,' he said, 'I imagine you know best.'

'Thank you for all you did, Mr Grainger.'

'For what? I haven't done nothing.'

'You helped me. You didn't ask why I came and you didn't make me leave.'

'That's what I say. I didn't do nothing.'

He nodded briefly and turned back up the drive. Imogen watched him go and then began the walk back to the village. Her cloak was still damp with last night's rain, heavy on her back. She was very tired, she realized.

When she reached home, she could hardly remember passing through the village. Whether anyone had been about, whether she had been seen. Scooping some water from the pitcher, she took a clean, cold drink and sat for a while at the kitchen table.

The light in the kitchen dimmed as someone came in from the yard and stood in the doorway. Her father. She recognized the scrape of his boots, the way he hesitated.

'Imogen?'

She didn't answer, but lifted her head a little to show that she'd heard.

'I've been out to look for you. I didn't know where you were.'

'I went for a long walk,' she told him flatly. 'There's nothing to worry about.'

'Good.' She heard him move behind her, clear his throat. 'Are you all right?'

'Yes, Dad. Just a bit tired.'

'Only, I found these,' he said, leaning over her and putting some pieces of pottery on the table. They rocked quickly for a moment, then settled.

Fortune. Broken in two along the line of the crack.

'Is this what you've been looking for?'

'Yes,' she said. 'Where did you . . . ?'

'He was in the yard, by the kiln-room. I don't know how he came to be there.'

She turned round, saw his hand on the back of the chair, and closed her own over it.

'I'll mend him, Dad. It'll be all right,' she said. 'I'm sorry if I worried you.'

'I was worried, Imogen. I've been walking around all morning thinking about things. Then, when I came back and saw your owl out there, I started to get a bit . . . frightened.'

'Frightened? What of?'

'I don't know. About losing you. You weren't in your room and I thought you might've . . . that you'd . . .'

'What?'

'Like I say. That I might've spoiled things and lost you.'

'No. You haven't, of course you haven't.'

'No,' he said and suddenly bent down to kiss the top of her head.